Praise for Avery Flynn's Books:

"Sexy and sassy... Avery Flynn brings it all."—*Carly Phillips, NY Times Bestselling Author*

"This book is so good you won't want to put it down."—*Harlequin Junkie, Enemies on Tap*

"Flynn intertwines fashionistas and fighters in book two of this heavily talked-about series and she'll leave readers breathless by the time they reach the heart-pounding finish."—*4.5 starts Top Pick, RT Book Reviews, This Year's Black*

Flynn knows her sass and sex ... sheer naughty fun!"—*Into the Fire author Amanda Usen, Betting the Billionaire*

"I loved this story."—*Darynda Jones, NY Times Bestselling Author, Jax and the Beanstalk Zombies*

"...Thrilling, funny passionate and even contains a few tips to keep the fashion police away from your doorstep."—*RT Book Reviews, High-Heeled Wonder*

Dangerous *Kiss*

(Laytons Book One)

By
Avery Flynn

Visit Avery's website at www.averyflynn.com.

Edited by KC
Formatting by Anessa Books

ISBN: 978-0-9908335-6-7
Manufactured in the United States of America

First Edition: 2011 (Temptation Creek)
Revision: May 2015 (Dangerous Kiss)

Dedication

To JGC for everything.

Acknowledgement

I couldn't have done this without the help of so many people including: the Lethal Ladies (and laddies), Avril and D'Ann, my crazy adopted family on PGL and, of course, the Tim to my Wilson. Thank you!

Author Note

Dangerous Kiss was first published in 2011 as Temptation Creek, but has since been revised.

Chapter One

*C*laire Layton readied herself to placate a dragon. Not a real one, of course; that would be easy.

But if Chef Carlos Alvarez had to be imagined as any kind of animal, the only answer was a fire-breathing, thick-scaled, roaring, flying beast.

The temperamental Guatemalan had holed himself up in Harvest Bistro's walk-in refrigerator. According to his sous chef, Dena, Carlos had screamed about the slow prep work and stormed off to pace amongst the heads of romaine and blocks of asiago cheese while chain-smoking skinny brown cigars and threatening to walk. If the health inspector heard about this, Claire couldn't imagine the fine. If the hundred customers restlessly waiting for their food in the dining room found out the chef was AWOL, she'd get run out of town on a rail.

Why were all chefs headcases? Her ulcer twitched in response to all the drama.

Whose stupid idea had it been to offer a gourmet, seven-course meal once a month on the night of the full moon anyway? Oh yeah, the Full Moon Special had been *her* brainchild.

She swiped a bottle of tropical-flavored antacids from the hostess stand and knocked back the fruity tablets like a Frat boy with a shot of cheap whiskey. She prayed Carlos hadn't yet graduated to rum.

Though eager to speed through the dining room in time with her panicked heartbeat, she forced her feet to slow down. She couldn't afford to spook the customers. Gritting her teeth, Claire pasted on a friendly smile and waved to the regulars, many of whom she'd grown up with in Dry Creek, Nebraska.

Seating was family style, with group tables for parties of less than eight. Folks had to drive five hours to Denver for anything close to the mouth-watering food she served during Harvest's Full Moon Specials. For the past six months during the full moon, every seat had been taken.

But tonight, one chair sat empty at table four.

A cute blonde, probably in her early twenties, sat next to the unclaimed seat with her cellphone glued to her ear, a gold charm bracelet glittering in the candlelight. Claire couldn't hear what the girl said as she fiddled with a small yellow piece of plastic. However, judging by the dirty looks the other diners at the table were sending the girl, they'd heard too much.

Pausing, she caught a nearby server's attention. "Kaylee, will you bring a bottle of house white to table four?" She pointed toward the girl. "They're starting to look restless and I have to talk Carlos back into the kitchen."

"Sure thing." Kaylee grimaced. "Good luck back there."

Straightening her shoulders, Claire girded herself for the battle that awaited her in the walk-in refrigerator. Damn, what else could go wrong tonight?

Six very long hours later, Claire glared at the trail of dark goo winding across the pointed toe of her gunmetal-gray stiletto. Call it Murphy's Law, fate or just plain old bad luck, but the last bag of kitchen garbage always leaked.

"Just great."

Holding the black plastic bag at arm's length, she strode across the deserted parking lot as fast as she could in four-inch heels. The kitchen crew had left at midnight, so at least no one saw her awkward rush to the Dumpster.

Thank God for small favors.

Eager to get home, Claire leaned in close to the chest-high Dumpster and pushed up the metal lid. Stink socked her right in the nose. Involuntarily, she recoiled, took a few steps back and held her breath. Sure, the garbage had been baking all day in Nebraska's blazing-hot August sun, but its putrid scent was worse than normal.

Never again would she make a bet with the kitchen staff that included garbage duty as the payoff. Carlos had giggled like a tween girl the first night he'd spotted her, the restaurant's owner, taking out the garbage. That had been a week ago.

Stupid soccer game.

Holding her breath, she heaved the dripping bag toward the gap. It plunked against the lid, bounced back and smacked her in the chest. Air whooshed out of her lungs. A glob of lukewarm mystery slime slid between her breasts and she squawked in disgust. Grossed out, she grimaced as she wiped it away.

Great. What a perfect way to end a busy Saturday night.

She couldn't wait to get home, rip off her dirty dress with its itchy label and kick her stained stilettos to the back of the closet. She hated those shoes, but pride shoehorned her into them. Her mammoth-size brothers had spent their lives teasing her about being one of the wee people. As a result, she made up the height difference however she could.

Changing into a tank top and yoga pants skyrocketed to the top of her to-do list. She'd grab a beer and head out to the deck to snuggle with her dog, Onion. Sure, she'd prefer cuddling with Mr. Tall, Dark and Amazingly Talented Between the Sheets, but he'd yet to appear naked in her bed. She'd thought she'd found him once. What a dud that cheating jerk had turned out to be.

Claire shoved the lid all the way open and hefted the bag into the Dumpster. The tension in her shoulders evaporated. Another Saturday night of work finished. Now it was time to relax.

As she reached around to close the lid, a golden glint sparkled in the moonlight illuminating the garbage bags. Curiosity piqued, she stretched herself as tall as her five-foot, two-inch frame could go, and leaned in for a closer look.

The scene registered like a grisly slideshow. A gold bracelet circled a thin, feminine wrist. The woman's hand, with short nails painted black, stuck out from underneath a worn plastic tarp. That tarp ran the length of the Dumpster and covered what looked like a body.

Claire yelped. Loud and high-pitched, her scream shattered the silence on Dry Creek's Main Street. Her stomach clenched and she whipped her head away from the Dumpster. Heart racing, she gulped in a deep breath of warm summer air.

Forcing herself to look again, she prayed the dim light and late hour had messed with her mind. With a jittery hand, she reached for the tarp corner buried underneath a pile of garbage bags. It crinkled as she pulled it from where it had snagged on the bracelet.

First, the rest of her arm appeared.

Then, tangled bleach-blonde hair.

Finally, a young woman's unblinking eyes stared back at her.

Claire scrambled away from the Dumpster

Hank. She had to call Hank. He'd know what to do.

But what if the murderer was still around? He could be watching her right at this moment. Her skin crawled and panic bubbled up inside her.

Crouching like a cornered animal, she scanned the parking lot for someone lurking in the shadows. A few crushed bushes with broken branches surrounded the lot. Dark liquid formed a small pool near the Dumpster. A newspaper skittered across the parking lot, pushed by the warm breeze.

Her jagged breathing echoed in her ears as her heart beat wildly. She was alone in the parking lot and danger seemed to hide behind every bush. It wasn't safe to call from here, she needed to seek shelter.

She'd be safe inside the restaurant. Once inside, she'd call Hank, snag a cast-iron skillet from the kitchen and play home-run derby on the killer's melon. Yeah, she could do that.

Her gaze jumping from one potential hiding spot for the killer to the next, she fumbled around inside her orange hobo bag for the keys to Harvest.

Sweat dampened the back of her neck and she couldn't catch her breath as she pawed through it. Anxiety tightened her chest, forcing her to work harder to draw in breath. Each second lasted an eternity. Pushed to the breaking point, her frustration peaked. Claire dumped out her bag onto the ground, foraged around in the resulting small mountain and grasped the keys and her cell.

Finally, the vise constricting her lungs relented. Her heart lifted and she hurtled toward Harvest's entrance. Until tonight, she'd never realized she could sprint in four-inch heels. All it took was the right motivation.

The click of the door's deadbolt sounded better than anything she'd ever heard in her life. It took two tries before she punched in the right numbers for the Dry Creek County Sheriff.

"Hey, sis, what can your newly elected county sheriff do for you tonight? Did you run out of gas again?"

Claire hunched over her phone. "Hank! Th-th-there's a gi-gi-girl in my Dumpster." Hysteria sharpened her voice. "She's dead, Hank. She's dead!"

"Okay. Calm down, Claire." In a heartbeat he turned all business. "Take a breath. Tell me where you are."

"I'm at Harvest. In-n-side."

"Claire, listen to me. Stay where you are. Don't let anyone in. I'm on my way."

"Hurry, Hank."

Despite the night's heat, a bead of cold sweat crept down the back of her neck and she darted a glance out the window. Though frightened to look, she found she couldn't turn away. A numbing stillness covered the parking lot. Even the breeze had stopped, as if it had been scared away. Inside Harvest only her panting broke the heavy silence.

The air conditioner clicked on with a whir and she nearly jumped out of her skin.

Get ahold of yourself.

Enough with the trembling at shadows and unexpected noises. Inhaling deeply, she tried to calm her jangling nerves. Freaking out wasn't doing her any good. If the killer hid in the parking lot, she needed to be focused and prepared to defend herself.

Clamping her jaw tight, she tucked her long hair behind her ears and flipped off her heels. Like a boxer before a big match, she bounced on the balls of her feet, flexed her fingers and rolled her shoulders back and forth. Her heart slowed and her hands didn't shake anymore. Well, not as much.

Time to get the skillet.

৩৩৩

Claire didn't loosen her white-knuckle grip on the omelet pan until Hank's cruiser squealed into the parking lot five minutes later. By then, she'd pushed the terror back with the determination of a soon-to-be bride at a seventy-five-percent-off wedding dress sale. Leaving the heavy cast-iron pan on the hostess stand, she hurried outside to meet her brother.

She kicked a twig from one of the mangled bushes out of her path. Harvest was the center of her world. No psycho would scare her away from her own restaurant, or its parking lot. At least not twice in one night.

She'd started Harvest three years ago with a small inheritance from Granny Marie and a massive loan from the bank. Her inability to boil water had killed her dreams of being a chef, but she wouldn't let that destroy her dream of owning her own restaurant. She'd lost buckets of sweat and tears to building Harvest up from the long-vacant remains of the abandoned Grand Hotel. For three years she'd spent nearly every waking hour here. Seven days out of seven, she was here for at least a few hours. Most days she arrived hours before the first line cook and left long after the final customers paid their bill. She couldn't remember the last time she'd gone on vacation, taken the day off to drive five hours to go shopping in Denver or even gone out on a date. Hell, she hadn't even had sex in forever.

Hank stood outlined by the glare of his cruiser's headlights. At six-feet, three-inches tall, with the sinewy bulk of a man who had played division one college football, he looked like a mountain compared to her petite frame. Hank, the eldest of her three brothers, took his duties as the oldest brother seriously. Normally, his protective temperament drove her nuts. Not tonight.

He strode toward her, a look of worry pasted on his face. "Are you okay?" Hank hugged her to him.

He held her so tight, one of his uniform shirt's buttons dug into her forehead. "I'm fine."

His tight grip overwhelmed her, emphasizing how vulnerable she'd been and how much she hated that feeling. Her frazzled nerves tensed, so she grabbed on to the one emotion more powerful than fear. Anger. Pushing away, she scowled up at him. "Really."

He tsked, obviously not impressed by her typical reaction to trouble, but let her go. "So tell me what happened."

Claire had to quicken her pace to keep up with his long stride. "I found her when I dumped the garbage."

"Did you see anyone? Anybody hanging around?"

"No."

"Lucky you." Hank towered over the Dumpster. Gripping his flashlight close to the bulb, he aimed it into the reeking depths.

A magnetic curiosity pulled her to Hank's side. She sidled up to him and raised herself on her tiptoes to see inside. The dead girl's lime-green eyes held no tears, but Claire found hers did. She blinked them away before Hank could spot them. If he realized how scared she'd been and how much seeing the dead girl affected her, he'd make her wait inside.

That wasn't going to happen. This was her kingdom. No one pushed her around at Harvest, even if it was declared a crime scene.

The dead girl must have been in her early twenties, probably a student at Cather College. Dressed in a flowery, turquoise sundress, she looked as if she'd been out for a night of fun with friends.

Blood matted her peroxide-blonde hair near her right temple. Not much, but enough to show how violently the girl's night had ended.

Again, Claire's gaze was drawn to the girl's gold charm bracelet. Pretty and delicate, it stood in stark contrast to its surroundings.

Realization hit her like a quick jab to the gut.

Earlier that night, the chatty girl at table four had worn a similar bracelet.

Could it be the same? The girl had ignored her fellow diners' dirty looks, aimed her way because she hadn't put her cellphone down for nearly the entire dinner service. Mostly she'd texted, but large gold stars had swung when she'd held the phone to her ear—the same gold stars now tarnished with discarded food scraps.

"Hank, I know her." Her voice sounded harsh in the quiet night.

He nodded, but didn't look up from the body as he snapped on a pair of latex gloves. "Who is she?"

"I don't know her name, but she ate at Harvest tonight."

Hank grunted in acknowledgement then started walking around the Dumpster. Every few steps he stopped, moving aside an old newspaper or other piece of debris with his foot. He'd taken about ten steps when he squatted by the Dumpster. Reaching behind, into the damaged bushes, he pulled out a crowbar.

Painted cherry red, it looked like the one she kept in her Jeep. He held it up in a gloved hand. Strings clung to one end of it. Claire squinted.

Hair. Bright, unnaturally blonde hair stuck to the end of the crowbar.

Her stomach roiled at the horrible sight.

Clutching her hand to her mouth, she stumbled away, not stopping until she reached the waist-high bushes bordering the opposite side of the parking lot. Afraid she'd hurl her dinner, she inhaled through her nose and exhaled out her mouth several times. As the warm breeze ruffled her hair, she pictured her happy place. A sparsely populated beach where the sun always shone. Fruity drinks with tacky paper umbrellas delivered by well-oiled and minimally dressed waiters. Waves rolling onto the shore in slow motion, tickling her toes buried in the white sand. After a few minutes, her stomach stopped flipping.

Turning, she faced her brother, who still stood by the Dumpster, and focused on how this could have happened.

How could someone have done this here? How could she not have known? What if she had taken the garbage out sooner, would she have caught the murderer in the act? Could she have saved the girl? Unable to answer any of the questions and frustrated by her powerlessness, Claire considered the facts.

The killer had left the body in her Dumpster. The girl had probably died here. Guilt rose like bile. She should have known something was amiss and stopped it, or at the very least called the cops. Harvest was her restaurant. It was her responsibility to protect her guests.

The bastard, whoever he was, would pay. She'd make sure of it.

She stomped back to Harvest's door, anger building with each step. Dry Creek was the kind of place where people said hi to each other when they passed on the street. They left their cars unlocked at the mall. To outsiders, it was just another railroad town on the flat Nebraska plain, but to the folks who lived here, it was home. Home was supposed to be safe.

Sure, they had crime, but it was nonviolent stuff. The mayor's house getting toilet-papered. A meth addict breaking into a house in the middle of the day when no one was home. Kids taking a car for a joyride. Nothing like this. She couldn't remember the last time there had been a murder in Dry Creek.

Hank's backup arrived in a convoy. Every deputy, on duty and off, flooded in while Claire glowered from Harvest's doorway.

They swarmed around the Dumpster. Some stood and gawked. Others talked off to the side with Hank. The CSI-type guys laid down numbered cards and snapped photos. Yellow crime scene tape spanned the entrance to the parking lot, resting on top of the bushes and trussing up her Jeep like a macabre Christmas present.

No way her Jeep was leaving the parking lot anytime soon. Great. How was she supposed to get home now?

She didn't want a deputy to give her a lift. She needed a friendly shoulder and a hug. Beth would come pick her up. It wouldn't be the first time she'd had to call her best friend at two in the morning, or been on the receiving end of such a call.

An invisible hand squeezed her brain like a sponge. Desperate for some aspirin to relieve her tension headache, she headed inside to raid Harvest's first-aid kit.

Her phone vibrated in her hand. Without even looking at the screen, she realized Beth's best-friend-sixth-sense must have kicked in. Either that or she was up late listening to the police scanner again. She'd gotten the scanner for Beth last Christmas. The girl had been addicted to it ever since. She could picture her now, curled up with a romance novel showing a bare-chested man on the cover, her ever-constant cup of coffee on the bedside table and the police scanner buzzing in the background. The idea made her smile for the first time in hours.

"Beth?"

"Sure, let's call me Beth," said an unfamiliar male voice.

Claire froze, ice-cold fear solidifying in her veins.

"I can see you right now, so pretend you're talking with Beth. That way none of the Barney Fifes end up with holes in their heads."

The deadly threat, delivered with a light touch, registered with finality. Her headache forgotten, she searched the crowd, looking for the Voice of Doom on the other end of the line. No one looked her way. No one held a phone. She spun on her heels and hurried toward Hank, toward help.

"Oh, Sugarplum, where are you going? No one can help you," the man taunted in his nasal tone. "And stop looking for me. People only see me when it's too late."

The phone slipped in her clammy hands, so she tightened her grip. Petrified, she tried to speak but only a choked coughing sound came out.

"Good girl. Now, I want her phone and flash drive. I want them immediately or you'll pay like she did."

Her body went numb. The phone fell to the ground and bounced off the asphalt. Claire gaped at it for a moment, her mind blank. Acting on instinct, she swooped up her cell.

Pressing the phone hard to her ear, she feared her shaking hands would drop it again. "Whose phone and flash drive?"

"Why, the dead girl's, of course, Ms. Klutz. I had hoped they were in her handbag, but I was wrong. I hate being wrong—it always means more work for me."

Desperate, she wished Hank would look at her. With this psycho's eyes on her, she couldn't wave her arms for help. She stared at the back of Hank's head. Muscles tense, she willed him to turn around. No luck.

"I don't have them." A tiny, naive part of her believed her pleading tone would work. He'd rescind his threat and life would go back to normal.

"Too bad. I'd hoped to do this without it having to get all messy—for you, that is."

His words blasted her fragile hope to pieces. Her only alternative was to get help. Someone else had to notice her distress.

"But you're lucky. It's late and I'm tired after, well, you know what I did tonight. Suffice it to say she had a lot more fight in her than expected." He chuckled.

At her wits end to find another way to gain someone's attention, she raised her voice. "Who are you? How'd you get my number?"

Engrossed in their jobs, no one glanced up. Defeated and alone in a parking lot filled with law enforcement, Claire sank down to the curb.

"Silly girl, I can read. Your name is on the menu as owner and proprietor. It doesn't take a genius to find a cellphone number. I love the Internet. Don't you?" He paused as if expecting her to answer. When she didn't, he carried on. "But, back to the matter at hand. I'll give you until noon to find what I want. You'll be hearing from me. And let's just keep all of this to ourselves, shall we? I'd hate to have to find a Dumpster big enough for you and your whole family."

The line went dead.

Chapter Two

*H*arvest's early lunch crowd's muffled chatter filtered up the stairs to Claire's office on the second floor. The sound barely registered in her worried mind as she paced across the tiny space. Pulse pounding, she chewed on her bottom lip.

Time was running out. Anxiety twisted her gut as she squinted at her laptop's clock. Her stomach dropped.

Eleven-thirty. Only thirty minutes left until the Voice of Doom's deadline.

Her purple kitten heels clicked across the hardwood floor, keeping pace with her frantic thoughts. Her nails dug into her palms as she fought against the panic boiling up inside her. The phone and flash drive had to be somewhere in the restaurant. Twenty-eight minutes left until the call. She still had time to find them. What had she missed?

The investigators never found a phone or flash drive in the Dumpster or on the body. She'd gotten that tidbit of information from Hank when she brought him coffee this morning. He'd leveled a strange look at her when she'd asked about it and the truth had almost bubbled out. But a vision of Hank's lifeless body pushed in with the garbage had stopped her cold. She'd deflected his curiosity by handing him a donut and skedaddled out of his office.

The poor girl had eaten here last night. Harvest was the only logical place the devices could be. She had to find them or the Voice of Doom would hurt her family. He'd already killed one person. Would a few more be all that difficult for him? Judging by the demented conversation they'd had last night, she guessed not.

Sitting down at her desk and letting her head fall to its solid surface, she rolled through the possibilities. She'd checked underneath all of the tables in the downstairs dining room. She'd sliced her hands through the booth seats' crevices and recovered about four bucks in spare change, a dozen gum wrappers and way too many bits of unidentifiable crumbly stuff. Nothing had lain underneath the upended fake potted plants. She'd looked behind the photos of area farmers that lined the walls. Nada. Her search of the kitchen had left her empty-handed. All she'd discovered after practically dismantling the bar was that she needed to order vodka.

Easing her head up from the desk, she gnawed her raw bottom lip. Her frustration festered as she tried to unwind the mystery. No ideas magically appeared. She couldn't envision any possible locations she hadn't already checked twice. Discarding each idea as soon as it occurred, a desperate tension built up with no release in sight. She spun her chair around, faced the window and berated herself for her lack of insight.

Always more comfortable with anger than fear, she focused on that emotion as she sought to answer the riddle.

"Hey there, Munchkin. Mom says hi."

In a single motion, she jumped up and whipped around. Her brother Chris leaned against the doorframe. The youngest and smallest of her three brothers, Chris stood six feet tall but compensated with a tall, black cowboy hat.

"No, Chris, you didn't call Mom." She groaned. "Why do all my brothers hate me?"

The last thing she needed was her mom to descend into this chaos. Glenda Layton would fuss and flutter around, pouring coffee for the deputies while whispering to Claire that none of this would have happened if she were married. Her mother meant well, but her constant harping for her children to get hitched and provide her with grandchildren drove them all nuts. Glenda wouldn't let a little detail like a murderer on the loose distract her from her life's mission. Claire was sure of it.

A look of mock innocence crossed Chris' face. "Oh, we don't hate you. We love to make your life hell. There's a difference."

Claire wanted to smack her head on the desk. Or, better yet, his head. "So what did she say?"

"Mom took it very well, I think. She said some words I didn't even know she knew. She and Pop are steering the RV out of Texas and back home to support the sweet baby of the family. So, if Pop maintains his cruising speed of forty-five miles per hour, they should be here in about three years." He didn't even try to hide the grin.

His sarcasm made her laugh. Tension drained away and her shoulder muscles loosened. Maybe all she needed to do to find the phone and flash drive was stop searching for them. That always worked when it came to finding her car keys. A quick cup of java downstairs and the answer would magically burst out of her subconscious. It would work. It had to.

"That's my Chris, always looking on the bright side. Come on, let's go downstairs and get some coffee."

"Yeah, about downstairs..." He stuffed his hands in his pockets and stared at the pine floor.

Her trouble meter flashed out a warning, sending heat streaming through her body. On edge, she gave her brother the stink eye. Chris' tone meant it could be anything from a coyote trapped in the kitchen to an angry mob protesting in front of the restaurant. Either way, it was bad news and she'd have to take care of it pronto.

"There's a dude downstairs sniffing around about what happened last night, and even if he is..."

Who in the hell would be digging up dirt? Sure, gossip was the lifeblood of a small town, but still, there was a dead girl involved and even the most callous rumormonger would wait a few days out of respect for the dead.

Maybe it wasn't someone local. It could be a reporter. The girl could have been a student at Cather College. You had to be pretty well-to-do to afford the small, private school's tuition. Maybe a reporter was hoping for a story that would boost his career to the big leagues.

A hot flash seared her skin. Maybe it was the Voice of Doom.

Panic danced on the edge of her thoughts. He'd said he'd call. Maybe the bastard had changed his mind? She opened her mouth to tell Chris, but a small voice warned her against it. What if it wasn't the killer?

There was only one way to find out. Claire marched out the door, intent on protecting her family.

The upstairs dining room's wall of windows had a great view of the revitalized downtown, including a 1940s-era movie theater. Usually Claire would slow down to admire the sight. Not today. She didn't even pause when she whacked her hip on a table. Swallowing a yelp of pain, she quick-stepped down the wide staircase, rubbing her aching hip.

Chris followed a few steps behind. "Claire, this guy is—"

"I'm about to find out exactly who he is."

A smattering of customers munched away at the round tables on the first floor. She didn't notice anything out of the ordinary. Well, except for the sudden drop in conversation followed by an immediate rise in the whispering.

Yeah, finding a dead body in your Dumpster will make people do that.

"Where is he?" Claire asked no one in particular.

Celestine Arthur, one of the regulars, pointed a bony finger toward the bar off to the side of the dining room. A malicious glow lit up the old crone's face.

"Enjoy the show, Celestine." Claire marched toward the side room, Chris hot on her heels.

Suzie, the bartender, stood behind the bar polishing it. Today, she had only one customer.

Target acquired.

Claire zoned in on the guy facing her at the opposite end of the bar. Steam floated up from the dusky orange coffee cup he palmed in his large hands.

He took a slow sip and his shoulders visibly relaxed. "Now that is a good cup of coffee, Suzie. Thank you."

His low voice slid over Claire's skin, caressing her hidden pleasure zones as strongly as if he had touched her. Unless he was a master at impersonations, there was no way last night's nasal-toned threats had come from the fine male specimen relaxing at her bar.

He must have felt the weight of her gaze because he raised his head.

Her breath caught. Damn, he was magnificent. He had close-cropped dark, almost black hair. She'd bet today's receipts that the small scar on his cheek was all that had kept his face from being plastered on billboards in Times Square. A small dimple in his chin punctuated his chiseled jaw. Only his full lips, almost feminine in appearance, balanced out the all-encompassing masculinity of the rest of his face.

He had trouble written all over him, the kind that made women of all ages yearn for a nearby bed. She licked her dry lips and stood as tall as she could.

As if accepting her positive appraisal as his due, he smirked and winked one of his slate-blue eyes at her. She snapped out of her trance. Pretty boys. They were all the same, self-centered jerks who looked like Apollo and acted like Hades. She'd learned that lesson the hard way.

So he wasn't the Voice of Doom. Who was he, and why was he in Harvest asking questions that were better left to law enforcement? Time to find out.

"I'm Claire Layton and I own Harvest. Is there something I can help you with?" Proud of her steady, almost neutral tone, she drummed her fingers on the gleaming bar.

The man sauntered over and stopped an inch shy of her toes. He was tall and so close. She inhaled his musky scent. His black shirt's buttons, level with the tip of her nose, worked valiantly to hold the material together across his muscular chest. Part of her hoped they'd burst just so she'd get a peek at the treasure beneath.

She forced her gaze upward. Her feet ached to take a step back, or forward, but she'd be damned if she'd give him the satisfaction.

"Who're you and what do you think you're doing in my restaurant?"

He laughed. Her nipples tightened at the warm, sensual sound. Her breath caught when he tweaked her on the nose.

"You're a spitfire, aren't you?" He chuckled, low and soft.

Her jaw nearly dropped to the floor. She couldn't believe it. He'd tapped her on the nose as if she were a five-year-old girl or a dog. An indignant flush swept up from her toes.

She managed, just barely, not to kick him in the shin.

"I'm Jake Warrick with Absolute Security in Denver. You must be Claire Layton, the girl who finds dead bodies in her garbage."

"Only one body, thank you very much." The words flew out before she could formulate a witty response.

"Yes, Kendall Burlington. Her father hired me to act as the family's eyes and ears during the investigation. They want to make sure everything stays on the up and up."

Claire's jaw jutted out at the insinuation about her brother's law enforcement ethics. Hank was the most ethical man she knew. He'd lock up his own mother before he'd be part of a cover up.

"Oh you, you..."

That's it.

Quick as lightning, her hand snaked across the bar. She snatched the water hose attached to the sink under the counter. With a flick of her wrist, she aimed the nozzle and let it rip.

The geyser soaked his shirt until it clung to his brawny chest.

Chris cut short her satisfaction, much to her dismay. Yanking the nozzle out of her grasp, he handed it to Suzie like a hot potato.

A wolf whistle blasted across the room.

"You better get that man a new shirt quick," Celestine hollered from the dining room. "Before one of the old biddies out here gets a little too excited seeing all those muscles."

Claire glanced over. Sure enough, Jake had peeled off his sopping-wet shirt. He did, indeed, have muscles on top of hard muscles. A dusting of dark hair covered his pecs. Her mutinous eyes followed the narrowing trail of hair until it dipped into the low-slung waistband of his jeans. She balled her hands to avoid reaching out and tracing the shadows on his six pack. Gritting her teeth, she forced her gaze to his face.

The bastard grinned at her. Her clit tingled in response.

Damn. Why did she always want the cocky jerks? There must be something wrong with her. She had to get out of here and give herself a chance to get her treacherous body under control.

"Chris, why don't you come with me to get a shirt for Mr. Warrick? We wouldn't want him to catch cold."

She stomped toward the storeroom.

৽৽৽৽

Jake winked at the interfering old lady in the dining room and sat down at the bar. Man, that water had been cold, even if the woman spraying it had been on fire.

What the hell had he been thinking, challenging her like that? He knew the rules. He had to win over the witnesses, gain their trust and charm them into telling him everything they knew. He'd just given the middle finger to every one of those requirements. What had this woman done to him?

She'd walked in with flames shooting out of the ends of her auburn hair, chocolate-brown eyes blazing. Dressed in a dark purple dress that wrapped around her tight body, highlighting her large breasts. His body responded to the fierce pixie. Strongly. He couldn't stop himself from stoking her inferno. Her heat had spread to him and turned any thought of his mission to ash.

A more cautious man—his father would say a smarter man—would have handled her gently. But he hadn't been able to do that. He'd had to push to see how hot she could burn.

Pretty damn hot.

Different time, different place and he'd let the fire run its course. But he couldn't do that today. He looked down at the bulge in his jeans. Looks like his cock hadn't gotten the message.

He sat down on the bar stool, trying to unobtrusively adjust his jeans. He reached over to where he'd been sitting and grabbed the worn leather satchel lying on the bar and pulled out the case dossier. His father had e-mailed it from Absolute Security's home office in Denver.

That's where Jake wished he was right now, waking up with the Rocky Mountains outside his window and a naked blonde in his bed, someone beautiful, tall and docile. Much more his type than Claire Layton.

He flipped through the printouts. Kendall Burlington, the very rich and spoiled adopted daughter of Denver hedge fund manager Charles Burlington, was the victim. Claire, the county sheriff's sister, had discovered Kendall's body in a Dumpster.

He wondered if the good sheriff had scattered any evidence to the wind on his sister's behalf. His gut told him she wasn't the killer, but she sure had a temper to go along with that red hair of hers.

She also had a redhead's tendency to blush, from her awe-inspiring tits to the top of her forehead. The memory made his cock rise. Again. Hell, he couldn't remember the last time he saw a woman blush.

An image of Claire arching her back, tossing her hair while she rode him, flashed into his head. Her nipples would be a dark rose color, he guessed. Her tits would sway with her rocking motion as she undulated on his erection. He'd grab her round hips, urge her to rock faster. She'd lean down. Her hard nipples would graze his chest as they kissed, their tongues curling around each other in an echo of what the rest of their bodies were doing. He'd flip her to her back, that red hair of hers spreading out across the white pillowcase like a sunset. She'd wrap her legs around him as he drove his hard dick into her wet center. He could hear her moaning, throaty and wanting. Then—

Whoa there.

She was a witness, not a candidate for making those fantasies a reality. He erased the tantalizing mental images and went back to reading the dossier.

Charles Burlington wasn't going to take any chances the case would go south because some local yokels couldn't investigate their way out of a paper bag. That's why he hired Absolute Security. Jake would poke his nose around without interfering with an ongoing investigation.

Earlier that morning, the old man had called saying Burlington wanted to know if the investigators had found Kendall's phone. The request stuck him as weird. She'd just been murdered, for God's sake, why zero in on her phone? Burlington had told the old man it had some photos Kendall's mother wanted. Jake figured grief made people focus on strange things. Still, the request stuck in his craw.

He scanned the initial sheriff's report. Nothing there about a phone. Where was it?

"She didn't do it, you know."

He looked up at the bartender.

"I've known Claire for years. She's not involved in anything bad."

Suzie, according to her purple, corncob-shaped name tag, wiped out a glass and set it on a shelf under the bar.

"People surprise each other all the time." He reached for his coffee. "You never know what's going on in someone else's mind."

He should know. He'd seen the pictures of his mother from when he was a toddler. She'd looked happy. His father thought she'd been content. But she hadn't been. No one had known until the day father and son came home to find all her clothes gone. A note had been taped to the fridge. *I want to be somebody new.*

They'd never heard from her again.

Yeah, people hid a lot about themselves. Who knew what secrets Claire hid behind her pretty face?

Chapter Three

Claire had to get Jake out of her bar. The hotshot from Denver pushed her buttons like a payphone.

Tongue tied and turned-on, her body and mind were in turmoil. She should have put a little more effort into getting laid before her whole world had gone crazy. Hell, she should have bothered to look at a man as dating potential. If she hadn't sworn off men, she wouldn't be worked into a lather over a yummy set of abs. And the way his appreciative gaze sent shocks through her. And how his voice turned her insides to jelly.

Chris walked ahead of her back to the bar. She stopped in the doorway and stared at Jake. Who wouldn't? With his movie star looks and granite-hard body, the man was beyond easy on the eyes and hard on the panties. Her body perked up, an electric shot of desire pulling her forward.

He sat at the bar, his attention on the papers in front of him. She savored the chance to observe him unnoticed. As he read, he seemed softer. Not weak, but less cocky and full of himself. However, a sense of restrained danger remained under the surface.

He reminded her of a black panther she'd seen once at the Denver Zoo. The creature had been powerful and languid at the same time. Even in repose on a wooden platform, the cat has a fluid, savage energy had surrounded the predatory cat. He'd swished his long tail and watched her from his perch. Despite the man-made moat and fence between her and the big cat, a chill had slid across her skin, warning of danger.

Jake looked up and caught her staring. In an instant, lust burned in his slate-blue eyes. He got up and stalked toward her, but Claire didn't feel like prey. No, this was a mutual hunt. She wanted to slide her hands through his short dark hair. Run her tongue across his washboard abs. Trail her fingers down his powerful back and over his hard ass. She couldn't help it. She couldn't explain it. She just wanted him. Badly.

The thought jarred her out of her fantasy. He was aggressive and obnoxious. She'd had enough of that type of man with her cheating ex-boyfriend, Brett. The next man in her bed wouldn't be some alpha male. He'd be caring, understanding and mellow. But man, she was woman enough to admit it would be a plus if he had Jake's Apollo-worthy bod.

Ugh, stop thinking about tying him to a bed!

She tried to ignore the need barreling through her body and dug her nails into her palms. The sharp pain distracted her from her impure thoughts. She breathed easier. Jutting her chin upwards, she put on her best superior expression, hoping it hid her desire.

"Here's one of the extra Harvest shirts. It's all we have."

She held out the dark-crimson T-shirt with the black Harvest logo. It hung from her fingertips in midair. Neither she nor Jake moved. The shirt dangled in front of him like a red flag waved at a bull.

The upward curl of his lips said he liked a challenge. A shiver slid down her spine.

When he took the shirt, their fingers brushed and a frisson of awareness shot up her arm. She jerked her hand back.

Jake wriggled his fingers, shook his head and pulled on the T-shirt. Watching the movement of his muscles as they bunched and stretched sucked her into fantasyland again. She forgot her annoyance and imagined wrapping her arms around his broad shoulders as he pushed her naked body against a wall. He'd set a slow and steady rhythm as she enveloped him.

A small groan escaped before she could stop the sound. The quirk of Jake's eyebrows forced her back to the present. Not that the view disappointed. The size large T-shirt fit tight across his broad shoulders. Against her better judgment, she regretted seeing his unyielding abs hidden away under soft cotton.

"I have to tell you, it's one of the more direct ways a woman has worked it so that I had to take off my shirt." He bent his head down toward her. "I didn't realize you country girls were so forward. Now, I don't mind you getting me wet, but next time, just ask."

Biting her lip, she fought the urge, again, to kick him in the shin. God, he was irritating. And enticing. And yummy to look at. And...oh God, this man erased all thoughts except those that involved him naked on her bed.

She flashed him an insincere smile and batted her eyelashes, hoping he wouldn't notice how her nipples had hardened. As if she'd said the words out loud, his gaze locked in on that exact part of her anatomy. Damn. They actually got harder.

She crossed her arms in front of her breasts. "Oh, I think once was enough. You know us country girls just aren't used to your big city ways."

"I could teach you about all things big." His wicked grin promised she'd learn a lot.

Electricity sparked between them, sank into her skin and settled low in her belly. "I'm sure you'd like to, but I'm not looking for a teacher."

That silenced him. He dragged his gaze from her toes to her eyes in slow motion. His hot perusal burned her skin as it traveled up her body, lingering on her breasts before stopping at her lips. A wolfish leer lit his face.

"I'm more than willing to be a student, if that's what you'd prefer," his voice rumbled.

Suzie squeaked and slapped her hand over her mouth. Fire burned Claire's face as another flush spread up her body. God, she hated her lack of control. Time to end this conversation before she ripped off his shirt and had her wicked way with him.

"Don't worry about bringing back the shirt. Think of it as Dry Creek's goodbye gift to you." She waved her fingers. "Have a safe drive back to Denver."

"But, I'm not going anywhere."

How did she know that was coming? And why did the buzzing sensation in her stomach intensify? Annoyed with him and herself, she shot him a black look. "Well, we're in a bar and you know the saying; you don't have to go home, but you can't stay here."

"Are you asking me to go home with you?" There was that smirk again.

She leveled her best "drop dead" look at him. Nothing happened. She'd used The Look to make late delivery men and handsy dates shake in the knees. It had never failed her. Until now.

The charged silence lasted another beat or two before Chris broke it. "So what is it you want to know?"

Jake's gaze hardened and never strayed from Claire. "I want to know how Kendall's body ended up in the Dumpster."

All of the desire flooding her body evaporated. Her chest tightened at the thought of Kendall and what misery her family must be going through right now. It made her heart ache to think of them. Even though her own family drove her nuts, Claire couldn't imagine what it would be like to lose a single one of them. And if a possible witness wouldn't take the time to share what they knew with an investigator? Well, that would horrible. She couldn't do that to the girl's family. They deserved better than to suffer more because of her hair-trigger temper.

Sighing, Claire sat down at the bar. "Honestly, I don't know. All I know is she was one of people with reservations last night."

Jake followed her lead, leaving an empty stool between them, and leaned in closer. "Did she come by herself?"

"Yeah, that's not uncommon for our Full Moon Special. That's the seven-course meal we have once a month on the night of the full moon. People make reservations in groups usually, but a few singles do too. We seat everyone family style. It's easier for the waitstaff that way because it limits the number of tables. Plus, it makes the meal seem more of a social experience."

"What was she like during dinner?"

She paused and looked up at Jake. His vibe no longer read as sexual. Instead of being full of heat, warmth and understanding beamed from his eyes, as if inviting her to share her confidences.

A girl could drown in those slate-blue eyes. Part of her wanted to. She shrugged off the wish, brought her attention back to the matter at hand.

"She didn't interact very much with the people around her. Whenever I checked on her table, she was either texting or talking on her phone."

"Phone?" Worry lines carved their way across his forehead. He shuffled through his papers on the bar. "There's nothing in the initial incident report about a cellphone being recovered. Sheriff Layton never mentioned finding Kendall's phone to her parents." He scooted his stool closer to her. "What happened to the phone?"

Claire straightened up so fast she almost fell off the stool. Her mind went into overdrive and adrenaline surged through her.

Phone.

Flash drive.

What time was it? She'd only been down here a moment. Right? She darted a furtive glance at the clock behind the bar.

Twelve-fifteen.

She'd missed the deadline. Her fear spiked. Her breath caught in her throat. The room grew hotter.

Automatically, she patted her dress pocket for her phone, but it wasn't there. She'd left it in her office.

She'd missed the Voice of Doom. Oh God, what was going to happen now? He'd call back, right? He wouldn't go straight in for the kill.

"What's wrong?"

Panic flooded through her body unabated. Her skin itched as if ants were doing the conga down her spine. If anything happened to her family, she'd never be able to forgive herself.

She had to get out of here, but couldn't bolt for the door.

She forced herself to concentrate on the bar, wiping at an imaginary stain. She couldn't let anyone suspect something was wrong. The killer had warned not to tell anyone about his call. But how to leave without causing suspicion?

"Hmmm? Wrong? Nothing's wrong. Why would you think something was wrong?"

She twisted her hair tightly around a finger and avoided looking at Jake. She jiggled her knee and fumbled for a way to get out of here.

"I asked about Kendall's phone and you went all squirrelly on me. What's the deal?"

She forced her body to be still. Jake didn't look as friendly. Now he acted like a dog angling to sneak off with the Thanksgiving turkey.

"Oh, nothing. Just remembered that some promised to call me. No big deal." She smi' tightly her cheeks ached.

"The look on your face says it's a big

She chewed on her bottom lip unti' stopped her. Damn. She'd been doin today. It hurt. "It's not, um, a big mean. For me, it's a, um, very, ve'

She mentally smacked her' Man, she sucked at lying. Ever as if she were some crazy lady. '

to drink? Suzie here makes a great iced coffee." Now she babbled.

She glanced at Chris, silently beseeching him for help. He looked at her like she had two heads. Suzie wouldn't even make eye contact.

"I'm okay. Now, about Kendall's phone, do you know what happened to it?" His tractor-beam gaze drew her in.

"It's not here at the restaurant." Ugh, why couldn't she just shut up?

"How do you know it's not at the restaurant? Did you look for it? Why would you do that?"

"Um, curiosity?" There went the nervous leg jiggle again.

He slapped his papers on the bar and leaned away from her. "Really? What was it about the phone that made you so curious?"

Her tongue stuck to the roof of her dry mouth. She couldn't think of anything that even remotely sounded plausible. No way could she tell Jake about the killer's threats. She couldn't risk her family. What could she say? Jake stared her down, making her feel about an inch tall. She wished he'd start talking again.

"I thought I might find you still here." Hank's deep baritone broke the silence.

He walked into the bar and tossed a set of car keys in her general direction. She caught them automatically. There were benefits to growing up with brothers, such as the no-look catch.

"Parked your Jeep in the lot. Sorry we had to it last night."

Hank fixed Jake with a straight stare. The two sized each other up. If either had a measuring stick, no doubt this was when they would have broken it out. Men.

"Sheriff Layton." Jake nodded toward the man in uniform.

"Call me Hank."

The statement was friendly. The tone was not. Hank didn't offer his hand to Jake in greeting. Either Jake didn't notice or he didn't care about the slight because he went on as if nothing awkward had happened.

"OK, Hank. I was just talking to your sister about Kendall's missing phone. It seems Claire was searching the restaurant for it. Did you ask her to do that?"

"No." He turned and looked at her. "Claire, why were you looking for a phone? And why did you ask me about whether we found one last night?" His testy tone was as effective as an interrogator shining a light in her face.

Both men stared at her. They had to know she hid something. What was she supposed to say? Maybe she should come clean? But where to start?

She weighed the benefits of telling versus killer's threats. Her palms became clammy. A reminder of last night's terrifying phone call. Once again, fear and panic boiled within her.

No one in the bar moved. Her gaze jumped one person to another before landing. Jake's face softened and he gave her an encouraging nod. She had to tell. Too much was at stake. For herself.

Harvest's assistant manager burst into the room, stopping in the doorway. "Claire!"

"Not right now, Jorge." She steeled herself for whatever the fallout would be for not speaking up about the phone call sooner.

"But, Claire, your Jeep is on fire."

Chapter Four

*H*eat slapped Jake across the face. From the doorway, he watched the Jeep burn like a bonfire in the parking lot. Claire gasped, then squeezed around him. They ran out the door, her brothers right behind them, and only made it a few steps before the crackling blaze's heat forced them to stop.

Orange flames stretched from the Jeep's now-crispy upholstery toward the sun straight above them. Benzene, smoke and burning vinyl seats poisoned the air around the gathering crowd of busboys, servers and curious customers.

What kind of life was Claire living? Could this be the work of a jealous ex-boyfriend, an angry customer, or had Kendall's killer picked out another victim?

Jake glanced over. She stood an arm's reach away, her bottom lip trembling. Then, she clenched her jaw tight. From the looks of her, she was either about to punch someone's lights out or bawl. The real fire had turned her feisty spark to ash.

The urge to tuck her into his arms and protect her from this latest disaster had him taking a step toward her before he stopped himself. He wouldn't get emotionally involved in a case, no matter how right it felt. Not a second time.

Shouts of, "Get the fire extinguisher," tore his attention away from Claire. A fire truck sped into the parking lot, drowning out the crowd's clamor.

Looked like there were benefits to living in a small town, and response time was one of them.

People moved back toward the bushes, giving the firefighters room. But one guy peeled off from the crowd. He didn't look forward. Instead, he kept his head down and turned slightly away. About six feet tall, he had shaggy, sandy hair with a skin-and-bones build. The man ignored the commotion as he made his way out of the parking lot.

The hairs on Jake's neck stood at attention. He didn't have any proof, but in his gut he knew. He leaned toward Hank.

"Sheriff, see the guy hoofing it out of here? White shirt? That's gotta be him," Jake said in a low voice.

In tandem, the two men strolled toward the suspect. Although adrenaline pumped through his veins faster than an avalanche in the Rockies, Jake had to stay slow and in control. A wrong move and he'd tip off the arsonist.

"You asshole! You set my car on fire!"

Claire's battle cry rose above the sound of the fire, the sirens and the crowd. He groaned as she streaked past him. Looked like she'd picked brawl over bawl.

As she chased after the suspect, the man booked it at a fast clip away from the banshee on his heels. Without hesitation Jake took off after them. He didn't think first, just followed her lead.

Damn, he seemed to do that a lot around this woman.

❧❧❧

Wrath. Pure, cold wrath overwhelmed Claire's better judgment. This guy had to be the Voice of Doom. Who else would blow up her car? After she heard Jake's comment, she tossed her kitten heels to Jorge and took off after the jerk.

Waif thin, the cretin didn't look as though he had the power to beat a girl to death. The thought of what he had done to Kendall and what he could do to her slowed Claire's pace for a moment, but righteous fury sped her back up.

She'd be damned if she let some murderer dump a girl's body at her restaurant, threaten her family, blow up her car and get away with it. If Hank and Jake weren't going to hightail it after him, she sure would. Letting him roam free meant a constant threat to her family's safety. She couldn't live with herself if the Voice of Doom hurt someone because she had missed his call.

But, damn, he ran fast.

The creep pivoted into the alley behind Harvest. He sped toward the railroad tracks a few blocks away. Something hard—she really didn't want to know what—pierced the bottom of her bare foot. Pain broke her stride, caused her to stumble.

She reeled. Flinging out an arm, she tried to straighten. She couldn't let him get away. Not when she was so close. Her shoulder banged against a Dumpster, making it throb but jolting herself back to an upright position. Recovering her balance, she ratcheted up her speed. Fear of him getting away spurred her forward.

She offered a silent thank you to her mother, who had forced her to join the track team in high school. Most mornings, she still ran for miles on the gravel side roads off Highway 28. Despite their quick pace, she hadn't even broken a sweat yet.

Digging deep for an extra burst of power, she pushed forward and got within reach. Hope filled her heart as she reached out. The bastard wouldn't be able to hurt anyone ever again. Her family would be safe.

Her fingertips brushed the sweat-soaked cotton of his T-shirt, but she couldn't hold on. He sprinted out of reach, looked back and sneered.

Oh, really? This guy didn't think she was a threat, huh? He'd learn. When it came to her family, she'd fight until the bitter end.

She blocked out the sound of her brothers hollering behind her as she ran and concentrated on her one goal, taking this guy down. An approaching train's blaring horn punched its way through her focus, planting an idea for how she could take him out.

One side of the alley dropped off into a short but steep, rocky embankment leading down to the train tracks. If she timed it just right, she could send him flying. Too much of a shove and she could lose her balance too. They could both end up on the train tracks with the engine bearing down on them.

She ignored her doubts and hammering heart. It would work. It had to.

Claire pushed herself to the limit, got within an arm's reach and launched herself at him. The unexpected impact forced him to stagger forward. Exactly what she wanted. But the momentum sent her with him, tumbling down the stony decline. Helpless to slow her descent, the surface as the world spun.

They rolled across the sharp rocks and slid to a stop just shy of the tracks and the oncoming train. She hurriedly unwrapped her twisted legs from around him, worried they had landed close enough for him to toss her into the train's path. They bounded up and faced off against each other as a train advanced. The locomotive's engineer blared his ear-splitting whistle.

Neither Claire nor the killer moved an inch. His nickel-size pupils were so dilated, she couldn't tell the color of his eyes. The fingers on his right hand twitched as he shifted his weight from side to side and ground his teeth. Drenched in sweat, he leered at her and an icy-cold dread spilled down her spine.

Her anxiety level ratcheted up about twelve notches. She'd seen it before, people tweaking as they came down off their meth high. It was the crack cocaine of the Midwest and he looked like the poster boy.

Not that she probably looked all that sane herself. Blood dripped from her battered elbow, her feet burned and she fought for breath. No way could she overpower him. She had to stall him until her brothers arrived. They'd beat this guy to a pulp. The thought made her downright giddy.

"Who are you and why are you doing this?" Claire hollered over the train clanking on the tracks.

He took a step closer, the stench of gasoline clung to him. "Everybody has bills to pay, Cupcake." He rushed at her and plowed his fist into her stomach, knocking the air from her lungs. He followed the shot with a quick jab to her face that rattled her teeth. Claire went down like a sack of potatoes.

"I want the phone and flash drive," he screamed down at her flat form, spit bubbling at the corner of his mouth. "You can't steal them from me. They're mine. She promised me!"

Gravel bit into Claire's back like tiny spikes. The rocks jumped and rattled next to her as the train barreled closer. She wanted to get up, but her muscles wouldn't budge. Her chest heaved up and down in a fruitless attempt to fill her lungs with air. Pain blurred her vision.

When was the cavalry coming? They hadn't run that far. Would they get here before or after this nut threw her onto the tracks to get scooped up by the train's cow catcher?

Why did she always react first and think second? She flipped from one possible outcome to another, each worse than the one before.

The sound of her name being yelled rose above the train's clatter. Thank God. She knew her brothers would come. They always did. She sucked in a painful breath.

This tweaker wouldn't get away. He'd pay for the damage he'd done. She hooked her arm around his ankle. Yanked. But he didn't fall. His swift kick to her stomach made her curl up in a spasm of pain. Without much effort, he tugged his leg from her grasp.

The Voice of Doom glanced up toward the alley. "You'll be seeing me again, Sweetheart." Then, as if it was no big deal, he jumped the tracks. He made it across right before the train passed.

Hot tears of fear and frustration slid down her cheeks. He'd be back. No doubt about it. If she couldn't find the phone and flash drive, her family would pay the price.

Claire sat up, slowly, despite her body's aching protests. The wind from the passing train whipped her hair into a halo of fury around her head.

Now that she could breathe again and the danger had passed, she took stock of her body. Her right cheekbone felt as though she'd been cracked with a hammer. Her scraped palms burned. Her bare feet throbbed, but the hard thing—whatever it was— had been dislodged from her sole.

"There's your silver lining." Claire rested her forehead on her knees. It wasn't much, but she needed something to go her way right now.

"What in the hell did you think you were doing? Do you have any idea how stupid that was? How dangerous? My God, Claire, you could've been killed," Hank yelled as the train's caboose receded from view.

She spied Hank at the top of the steep embankment with Jake and Chris. Chris wore a grim frown that matched Hank's scowl. Jake looked toward the horizon, past the train tracks. Glancing back, she confirmed the killer had disappeared onto Dry Creek's unsuspecting Main Street.

She shaded her face against the midday sun. "Aren't you at least going to help me up?"

Hank glared down at her. "You ran after some guy who probably set your Jeep on fire. Get your own damn self up."

With that bit of surly brotherly love, he turned and stomped away. He hadn't made it three steps before he stopped, looked skyward, grumbled something Claire knew she didn't want to hear and came back.

Hank and Chris half slid, half stumbled down the embankment. Each brother grabbed one of her arms and hauled her up. Angry and embarrassed about her imprudent chase, she stared at the ground.

"Are you OK?" Chris asked close to her ear.

She brushed the muck off her dirt-streaked wrap dress. "Besides my car blowing up, having the wind knocked out of me and getting punched in the face? Oh, I'm fine."

Relief swept across his face like windshield wipers sweeping away the rain. His usual smart-aleck grin returned. "Good. I'll be sure to let Mom know you're OK when I call to update her on this latest fiasco of yours."

"Chris, you call her and I'll...I'll...I'll do something you won't like," Claire sputtered.

Chris grinned like an overjoyed hyena. He'd been impervious to her nasty looks since birth. They'd been playing this game for years. One would get in trouble and the other would tease and prod to relieve the stress. It had always worked in the past, so why was she still so pissed?

She shook off her brothers, who both stayed near the train tracks. Holding her battered arms out to the sides and hunching forward to aid with balance, she made her way up the steep embankment. The sight of two tan workbooks sent butterflies spinning throughout her sore torso. With a sigh, she came to a stop in front of Jake. He stared down at her, their height difference made even more dramatic because she was shoeless and still a foot down the embankment.

"You are a dangerous woman to know, Claire Layton." He shook his head. "Still, you gotta admire someone who goes after what she wants. Here." He held out his hand to help her up the final few steps.

She hesitated, entranced by the muscles in his outstretched arm. His wide hand with its heavily lined palm enticed her. He crooked a long finger and motioned her forward.

A secret part of her heart stuttered. This man was trouble. Her stomach buzzed. Her breath shallowed. Her bra tightened around her tender breasts.

Jake's smirk slid away, replaced by ill-disguised lust. He strode down to her, curled an arm around her waist and scooped her up. He carried her the last few steps up to the alley.

It felt too good to protest. Her aches and pains lessened in his strong arms and she forgot her scraped elbow and sore jaw. Hell, she barely recalled she had feet, let alone the throbbing on the bottom of her foot from moments earlier. Instead, her waist tingled where his arm touched her. She soaked in the heat emanating from his hard chest.

Any frustration at her ability to fight against this attraction vanished as she melted in his embrace. Her whole body relaxed into his.

Staring at the Harvest logo on Jake's borrowed T-shirt, she tried to get her body back under control. Where had all this come from? She didn't even know this guy.

It had to be adrenaline. Right? Yeah, this was all the effects of the adrenaline rush. It had nothing to do with something special about him.

"Thank you for your help but you can put me down now." She pushed against his chest. She needed space between their bodies.

"I don't think I'm ready to do that."

She raised her head at his strained tone.

All the words in her head disintegrated. She doubted she even remembered her own name. All she wanted to do was stay right here in Jake's arms. Preferably naked. Maybe on a bed, but that wasn't a requirement.

He tightened his arm around her waist, pulled her in closer to his hard body. Jake leaned his head down but stopped when their mouths were only an inch apart. His breath fluttered against her lips.

"If you keep looking at me like that, we're both going to regret it," he ground out.

She leaned her head against his shoulder and wished the rest of the world would disappear. Graphic images in glorious Technicolor flashed through her thoughts, making her breasts heavy. Moonlight casting shadows on his six-pack abs. Rubbing up against him while skinny dipping. Feeling his calloused fingers squeezing her ass as she slid down on his hard cock.

She didn't want to let the fantasies go, but whoever said life was easy? He was here today and gone tomorrow. Not her kind of man. She wanted more.

"You wish He-Man. Put me down." She'd tried to make her voice sound gruff, but it came out a hoarse whisper.

She felt his sigh more than heard it. The slight rise of his chest made her curl her fingers into his T-shirt, take in a last whiff of his cologne. She couldn't place it, but it reminded her of dark rooms and unleashed desire.

After a moment's hesitation, he lowered her until she stood on the asphalt.

A jolt of pain shot through her right foot. She gasped. Balancing on her left leg flamingo style, she examined the one-inch gash on the ball of her right foot. She flashed back to the hard thing she'd stepped on.

"Great." She'd have to hobble on one foot back to Harvest.

Chris scrambled up the embankment. He stopped beside her.

"That's nasty. God knows what you stepped on out here. What kind of person runs in an alley barefoot?" He peered closer at her face. "Oh, and your eye is starting to puff up. Nice."

She flipped him the bird. Immature? Yes. Satisfying? Uh-huh.

Hank stepped into the alley and held up a folded piece of paper. "I found this near the railroad tracks."

They crowded around Hank. He unfolded the grimy square to reveal a younger Kendall Burlington. She smiled shyly up at them. It looked like a copy from an old yearbook photo. Her then dishwater-blonde hair hung in a low ponytail. She wore a strand of white pearls and a black, scoop-necked dress.

"Why would the Voice of Doom kill her? She looks so sweet," Claire said quietly.

All three men turned to stare at her.

"The Voice of Doom? Who the hell is the Voice of Doom? And what kind of dumb name is that?" Hank asked.

"I had to call him something. Whacked Out Killer Who dumped a Body in my Dumpster seemed a little too long." Claire twisted a strand of hair around her fingers. She had to tell them about the call and the threats. This would not be fun. Hank would be irate that she had held it back from him. Who knew what Jake would think? She felt like crap already, best to get it over with.

She took a deep breath, then told them about the call and the demand for Kendall's flash drive and phone.

"I was going to tell you all of this at Harvest, but then my car got blown up."

"You knew all of this and took off after this guy anyway?" Hank smacked his head with his hand as he hollered. "Do you have some kind of death wish?"

"Hank, stop acting like my older brother for a minute. We have proof this guy is tied to Kendall. Isn't it worth something?"

"It's not worth your life."

The worried look on Hank's face shut her up. She'd scared him when she'd run after the killer. To be honest, now that the adrenaline had leaked out of her system, her reaction frightened her, too. She hadn't thought first, she'd let impulse rule her actions. Again.

She wouldn't actually tell Hank she had acted reckless. No, confession went against the little sister code. Instead, she hobbled over and gave him a hug. He squeezed her back. She was sorry. He understood.

"All right, all right. Enough PDA here." Hank gave her a quick peck on the forehead and headed toward Harvest.

She shuffled, hopped, shuffled down the alley to keep her weight off her injured foot. It felt like she'd been stung by a bee the size of a mountain lion, but wouldn't cripple her for life.

Hank, already ahead, didn't notice her discomfort, but Chris did. He hunkered down. "Piggy back?"

She awkwardly pulled herself up onto Chris' back. Glancing back at Jake, she saw he hadn't moved. A look of stark yearning lay bare on his face.

For her? For her crazy but loving family?

He caught her staring and the emotional display disappeared. He ran his fingers through his short black hair and looked into the distance.

A pang of regret squeezed her chest.

Wrong time.

Wrong man.

She needed...well, no one right now. Not after Brett. She'd sworn off men for at least a year. Add to that her three interfering brothers and the last thing she wanted was another man who thought he had to protect her and guide her. For too long she'd let the men in her life do just that.

෧ৡৡ෧

An hour and two cups of coffee later, the firefighters were gone but the stench of burnt Jeep remained. Its carcass dripped in the afternoon sun, a bizarre centerpiece in Harvest's parking lot.

Damn, Claire had loved that car. She'd miss the feel of the wind blowing through her hair on the twenty-minute drive home while she blasted the satellite radio.

"Mourning the Jeep?"

Sitting on the employee bench outside the back door, she shaded her eyes with her hand and looked up at her brother. Chris held an industrial-size brown bottle. She squinted at the label. Hydrogen peroxide. He'd wanted to distract her with his question. Really, it was kind of sweet. She would have told him so too, if he hadn't chosen that moment to yank her foot out and pour the clear liquid over the small gash. It bubbled and hissed like he'd just opened up a shaken Coke bottle. She jerked her foot out of his hand.

"Hurts like crazy, doesn't it?" Chris twisted the cap back on the bottle. "Mom always said the sizzle means it's working."

"Give me the stupid bandage."

He slapped it into her outstretched palm.

"I'll be right back." He paused right outside Harvest's door and waved the bottle at her. "Unless you want another shot of the good stuff."

She would have hurled something at him if there had been any ammunition nearby.

Chris had always been a tease, winning the super lottery hadn't changed him a bit. Except now he had more time to be annoying.

She pushed the sticky ends of the bandage onto her sole. The icy burn from the hydrogen peroxide subsided. Bandages always made injuries feel better. True at age eight and still true at twenty-eight.

"At least let me take you home." Hank slapped his dark brown sheriff's hat against his thigh.

Claire slid her sore foot into her shoe, stood up and bounced gently to test her pain threshold. It ached, but nothing she couldn't handle.

"Hank, I appreciate the offer. I really do." She smoothed her skirt, hopelessly marred with dirt. "But I drove the farm truck in this morning and if you took me home, I'd be stuck out in the country without transportation. Anyway, the Voice of Doom knows I don't have the phone or the flash drive." She didn't think he'd buy that last bit, but she had to try.

She took in his disapproval, evident by the set of his jaw. He glared at her. The vein at his temple pulsed as he gnawed on an already tortured nail. As the eldest brother, he'd always been her first and most effective protector. No surprise that he'd gone into law enforcement.

"That's crap and you know it." He spit part of his nail to the ground.

"Look, I'm only going home for a few hours to shower and let the dog out. I'll be back before the dinner service. And despite what you think, I'm not completely without defenses. I've got dad's quail-hunting guns at the house. You know damn well that I'm a good shot."

He regarded her without comment. She gave him her best everything-will-be-okay smile. Hank shook his head and walked away. A few minutes later, he and Chris took off in their cars.

She didn't know where Jake had gone. She surreptitiously looked for him for half an hour with no luck before she got behind the wheel of the decrepit farm truck to head home.

The truck had a hole in the passenger-side floorboard, dents and rust along both sides and an arthritic manual transmission. Her parents had sold a large part of the family farm to finance their post-retirement dream of cruising around the country in an RV. However, her father refused to part with the heap of a truck. He'd left it parked in Claire's garage—something she was grateful for this morning when she'd needed to get into town.

But now, she couldn't wait to get home and shower. She planned to break out the double chocolate fudge ice cream for a quick dinner. Healthy? No, but after the day she'd had, she deserved a little bad-food loving. Claire turned the key in the truck's ignition.

Nothing. Not a groan of the engine. Not a click of the starter. Nada.

She tried again. Still zilch.

After everything that had happened today, she had to deal with a non-responsive engine, too? The addition was more than she could take. Her temper exploded.

She stomped her feet on the pedals. Yanked on the immobile steering wheel. Cursed and railed against the unfairness of it all. She was in the middle of a diatribe about how the truck would be sorry when it went up for auction at the scrap metal dealer's when a chuckle interrupted her tirade.

Slowly, already knowing who it was and hating that fact, she turned.

Jake stood outside the truck's passenger door. His right elbow rested on the open window frame with his chin cradled in his palm as if he were enjoying the show.

"Need a ride?" He winked.

Chapter Five

The SUV crunched over the gravel drive to Claire's house and lurched to a stop. She cracked her eyelids, and through the slits she spied the cornfield surrounding her house on three sides. The field blazed golden in the late Sunday afternoon sun, welcoming her home.

Relief wrapped around her like a warm blanket. Not that chills were her problem. No. Being trapped in a car for twenty minutes with Jake had kept her plenty hot and more than a little bothered. She couldn't wait to get out of his SUV and send him on his way back to town.

When she had climbed into his gas-guzzler, her brilliant plan had been to ignore him on the ride home. Things were crazy enough right now without adding her lustful thoughts about him to the mix. Too bad her scheme hadn't worked

She'd given him directions to her house, leaned her head against the window of his black SUV and faked sleep to avoid talking. Rude, yes, but her options were limited and jumping his bones wasn't an one of them. Unfortunately, her lack of sight had only enhanced her other senses.

The musky scent of his cologne had teased her as her body vibrated in time with the SUV's motor. Hyperaware, her muscles had tensed every time he'd moved in his seat.

He had started singing along to an old Smoky Robinson Motown tune. His golden tenor had softened her resolve to ignore him as he had sung, "I don't want you, but I need you. Don't wanna kiss you, but I need to."

She'd squeezed her thighs together to maintain her balance with every twist and turn in the road. The pressure had built in her clit until she'd surrendered to her naughty imaginings. He would sing as he kissed his way down her stomach, a day's growth of beard tickling her. He'd stop at that spot right below her ribs. Kiss his way across the flat plateau, grasping her hips tight to keep her from wriggling too much. He'd linger near her bellybutton before veering lower and crossing over to her right hip. She'd arch her back, silently beseeching him to move toward her wet pussy. He'd murmur the song's lyrics as his mouth traveled toward her shaved lips.

Just as her daydream was about to pay off, his SUV had jerked to a halt.

As he cut the motor, she squeezed her thighs together to ease the throbbing pressure. The squirming didn't help.

"What in the world is that?" His jaw dropped as he stared at her house.

Ignoring the desire pulling her body taut, she glanced out the front windshield. And like that, the invisible weight on her shoulders evaporated.

The dog spotted her and went nuts. He wiggled from the tip of his snout to his tail. He circled. He yipped and whined.

She shrugged and opened the door. "That's Onion." She jumped down to the driveway and snuck a sideways glance at Jake. He sat slack-jawed behind the wheel.

Her dog galloped to her side. No one could beat Onion in an ugly dog contest. He looked like a drunken, mad scientist had fashioned him from the leftover parts of several mangy mutts. He had a Bulldog's short, muscular body, a Chow's fluffy, curled tail and a few black spots dotted his tan coat. A Labrador's endearing personality topped off the package. Yep. Onion was an unsightly mess. But she loved him.

She bent and scratched him behind the ears. "What are you doing out here, you silly dog? How'd you sneak out this time?"

Onion looked ugly, but he had a beautiful brain. The dog got into or out of anywhere he wanted. She'd tried to crate him once. He'd escaped before she'd even pulled out of the drive.

"I think he just walked out the front door," Jake said, slamming his car door shut and walked over to her side.

Claire scrutinized the wraparound porch. Sure enough, the front door hung wide open. She took a step forward, but Jake grabbed her elbow, tugging her to his side.

"Where do you think you're going?"

She yanked her arm. "Inside my house."

He jerked her around so she was behind him as he scanned the area. "How'd that work out for you last time you took off without thinking first?"

She wanted to tell him how wrong his words were. But she couldn't. He was right. A fact that annoyed her to no end.

"He could be in there." Jake waved toward the house. "He could be armed."

"I don't think Onion would be acting all lovey-dovey if that maniac was here. He's not a doggie model, but he's smart. He probably scattered as soon as trouble hit and has been waiting for me to get back."

Jake looked down at Onion, who busily sniffed his boots. He patted the dog's head. Grudgingly, she chalked up a point in his favor for being nice to Onion.

"OK, but stay with me and don't do anything stupid."

The urge to get inside overrode her need to make a snappy comeback. She didn't like it, but she wasn't going to argue the point.

She and Jake sidled up the steps to the wide front porch. The door's stained-glass center oval had been shattered.

"I'm beginning to think I'm cursed," she said.

Jake clutched her hand in his, sending a jolt of awareness up her arm. "I'm beginning to agree." Together, they tiptoed around the glass and through the open doorway.

Once inside, Claire stifled a scream.

The sicko's tornado of evil had left a destructive wake through the 1900s-era farmhouse. She wanted to pitch a fit and throw things. Too bad the Voice of Doom had already done the job for her.

He'd thrown open the kitchen drawers and tossed the spoons and forks onto the tile floor. She found books that had been thrust off shelves and thrown across the living room. In the dining room, broken family pictures lay whatever they'd landed, glass shards decorated everything. She couldn't take more than a few steps into the office because of the wreckage there. Dresses, shirts jeans, tank tops and socks littered her bedroom floor. A pair of hot-pink lacy panties hung from the ceiling fan. If she wasn't so mad, she would have been embarrassed about Jake seeing that.

"Claire! Get in here."

She hustled back into the kitchen. Jake stood in the pantry's open doorway, his back to her. His bulk blocked her from seeing inside and she nudged him with her elbow. Without looking her way, he shuffled sideways.

A gas canister sat in the middle of the pantry floor, its fumes wafting out of the doorway. A bright blue bow was stuck to the handle. The killer had left a message in Easy Cheese next to the gas can.

See you soon.

She hated the fear growing inside her. Being frightened never helped anything. It got in the way. Stopped her from doing what needed to be done. But not this time. Too much was at stake for that. She'd have this guy's head on a pike.

"The bastard is going to fry." Her trembling lip betrayed the bravado in her words. "No way is he burning down my house. I'll be waiting when he comes back. "

"Want company?"

Claire took stock of Jake's muscular frame. This fight required more than brawn. "You any good with a gun?"

"You bet." His cold grin didn't reach his eyes.

"This asshole already threatened my family."

"Good thing I'm not family."

She chewed her sore bottom lip. "One condition. You can't tell Hank about the gift in the pantry." She nodded toward the gas can.

"He's the sheriff. He should know."

"He will, but not now. Hank has to play by the rules. This psycho doesn't. I don't."

Jake didn't speak for a minute. "Fine."

Relief flooded her body. She didn't want to face off against the Voice of Doom alone.

"OK. Let's see what else the jerk left behind before you call Hank. But when you do, leave this part out."

"Shouldn't you call him?"

She eyeballed him. "If I call, he'll pester me until I tell him every little detail. I haven't been able to keep a secret from him for longer than twenty minutes in my whole life. You need to call."

"Yes ma'am." He gave her a mock salute. She huffed out a breath that sent a few tendrils of hair flying from her face and left to assess the damage in the rest of the house.

Claire's fury swelled each time she heard a crunch underfoot or felt the ragged edge of something that used to be whole. The psycho was lucky she didn't find him crouched behind the shut shower curtain because she would have beat him with the curtain rod.

She couldn't remember when anger had become her default mode when faced with adversity. Probably soon after she'd found Brett and some tall blonde passed out naked in her bed. In response, she ran. She stayed busy. It worked. Mostly. She picked up the shattered frame that held her college graduation photo and wondered if somewhere inside her that trusting, optimistic girl still lived.

"All clear," Jake hollered from another part of the house.

Today was not the time to find out. She stalked out to the porch and armed herself with a broom and a sour attitude. Picturing the killer's face in each glass splinter and particle, she swept the sharp pieces into a mound.

Granny Marie's grandmother had gotten that door shipped all the way from Kansas City. Four generations of Layton women had basked in the jewel-colored light streaming from it. Claire use to play Barbies in its colorful shadow. A few years later, she'd had her first kiss sandwiched between the door and Bobby Carr's lean, teenage body. When she came home with her heart shattered by Brett, seeing that door had made everything better somehow.

Firebombing her Jeep was one thing. Destroying Granny Marie's stained-glass door was something else.

A shadow fell across her path. Jake pried the broom handle from her grasp and held out his cellphone.

"Hank wants to talk to you."

She backed away as if he'd pointed a lit firecracker right at her. Despite the phone being a foot away, Hank's cursing came through loud and clear on the phone's tiny speaker. She swiped it out of Jake's hand and held it away from her ear.

"Stop cussing at me, Hank, or I'll hang this phone right up."

Silence greeted her declaration. It lasted so long she feared he'd hung up on *her*. "Hello?"

"Fine." He snorted. "You have to get out of that house now."

"No."

"No?"

She yanked the phone away from her ear. People in the next county must have heard Hank's booming rant that followed. Jake cocked his head to the side. She shrugged her shoulders.

"Hank," she hollered into the phone. "He's not here. It's okay."

"No, it's not okay."

"Look, I won't let this nutcase turn my life upside down anymore. Come out and take a report if you have to, but I'm staying put." She fumbled for the end-call button on the unfamiliar phone.

Taking in a deep breath, she closed her eyes and counted to twenty. Then she counted to forty. By the time she'd gotten to sixty, she felt better. She lowered her body down to the top step next to Jake and handed him his phone.

Gazing out at the neighboring field, she watched the corn's yellow husks dancing in the wind. A year ago, she'd returned home heartbroken with her self-confidence obliterated. Granny Marie, already ailing, fixed up Claire's old bedroom and nagged her until she finally ate. She'd brought Claire back to the land of the living right before Granny Marie left it. On her deathbed, Granny Marie made her promise to keep the family home.

She'd done a hell of a job.

"You know he's only trying to keep you safe."

"Yeah, I know."

Onion wriggled in under her arm, squeezing his big body onto her small lap. She stroked the stressed-out dog's head and enjoyed the silky smooth fur against her fingers.

The killer wanted that phone and flash drive. He thought she had them. She wished like hell she did.

She'd give him the damn things in a heartbeat, just so he'd go away. Groaning, she laid her head on Onion and inhaled his scent of dirt and dog sweat.

"You know, you really might want to consider a maid if you're too busy to pick up after yourself."

Jake's face gave nothing away. No smile crinkled the corner of his eyes. His lips never twitched upward. He didn't even look at her.

It took a second for the deadpan humor of the statement to filter through to her. When it did, she laughed. Loudly. The sound roared out of her body with such gusto, it released the pent-up anger and anxiety formerly settled like concrete in her stomach.

"Thanks. I needed a laugh." Without thinking, she gave his shoulders a quick squeeze. She meant it to be a friendly gesture, but when they touched, something inside her clicked into place.

"Yeah, I picked up on that, being a crack investigator and all." He patted her leg, and left his hand resting on her thigh. His calloused thumb sent tingles shooting through her body.

His hand captured her attention. Long, lean fingers. Close-clipped nails, except for the thumb. That nail looked as if it were a regular afternoon snack. His tan palm covered the width of her leg. Warmth surged through her limb to the rest of her body.

"You sure do make it hard not to like you."

His finger traced tight circles on her thigh. "Well, they say everybody has a talent."

Onion crawled across her lap and squashed Jake's hand to her thigh. The dog laid his front paws on Jake. He rubbed his wet snout across Jake's free hand, demanding a pet. When Jake obliged, Onion whapped Claire in the face with his wagging tail.

"Guess you can't be all bad. Onion likes you." She pushed down Onion's dancing tail. Her gaze caught Jake's.

The silence sizzled. There might be more to this man than she first thought. Maybe her body knew something her mind had yet to grasp.

She lost her train of thought when Onion's back paws dug painfully into her stomach. He leaped down and barked at the dust cloud kicked up by two vehicles traveling the dirt road to her house. As they rolled closer, her gut tightened.

Onion barked incessantly as if his mortal enemy, the UPS truck, had pulled into her driveway. But instead of the big brown truck, Hank's cruiser led the way for a Volvo sedan.

"Just great." She walked down the steps. "Follow my lead."

Hands on her hips, Claire scrutinized the trio of Layton men in her driveway. If Hank was the bossy brother and Chris the big-hearted goof, then her middle brother, Sam, claimed the title of most uptight. A history professor at Cather College, he smiled little and laughed less. It did not bode well that all three brothers had joined forces on her front lawn.

She fired the first volley. "I already told you on the phone that I'm staying here. I'll be damned if I let this guy scare me out of my own house."

That stopped the men's approach. Jake remained silent on the porch. Onion, oblivious to the tension, sniffed every last scent out of her brothers' pants. She stood her ground.

"You mean you're staying to guard the house with the broken front door?" Sam nodded toward the few stained-glass shards still clinging to the splintered door.

"That can be fixed. I have plywood in the garage. Anyway, Jake's staying with me."

Sam pinched the bridge of his nose between his thumb and forefinger. "Oh, that is so much better. The two of you are going to stay here, with an oh-so-secure plywood front door while some...some...psychopath is out to get you?" He took a step forward. "That's a great plan. A perfect plan. Why don't you just let us know where your will is, so we can take care of things after this guy kills you."

That stung. She'd always sought his approval above all others. The hurt bubbled up, her throat tightened and her stubborn streak widened at least a mile.

"Samuelson Aaron Layton, that was a mean thing to say." Something in her quiet voice must have called out to Onion. He lopped over and sat with his body pressed against her leg. "I've made my decision and I'm sticking to it. I won't concede victory to the Voice of Doom."

"The Voice of Doom? What is he, a cartoon supervillain?" Sam looked heavenward. "I swear you're more obstinate than is good for you. For once in your life, think, don't react."

Chris, ever the peacemaker, strode up to Claire and blocked her line of sight to Sam.

"Claire, I think what Sam is trying to say is we can't sit by and watch you risk your life. We love you." Chris paused for a breath. "Anyway, Mom would force-feed us nothing but steamed broccoli for a month of Sundays if anything happened to you."

She chuckled at that. She didn't know how he managed to do it, but Chris sucked the tension out of a situation better than anyone else in the world. God, she loved him.

Really, she loved all of them. But they had to learn she could take care of herself. She'd graduated from college, earned her MBA, had her heart pulverized and started her own restaurant, a successful one at that. Was it a baby sister thing? Was it a girl thing?

Who knew and who cared. It ended now. Today, she took care of *them*.

Her fingers trailed through Onion's fur, causing his tail to thunk on the ground.

"Thank you all for coming out. I appreciate your concern, but I'm fine. Hank, let's get that report over with." She glanced back at Jake still sitting on the porch steps. "My fridge is empty. Do you mind going into town to grab a pizza?"

Jake ambled over to her side. "Sure. What do you like?"

"Everything."

The smirk returned. "My kind of woman."

Chapter Six

$\mathcal{J}$ ake had no clue how he'd ended up as the pizza delivery boy. He'd started off the afternoon as the valiant protector. Now he sat in the King Pizza parking lot waiting for a large pepperoni. The scent of warm grease did little to distract him from the redhead who had somehow submarined his free will.

Claire said jump and he asked how high. And he liked it. Damn. The old man would be calling him six kinds of a wimp if he knew, but he couldn't put off checking in with his father any longer.

"'Bout damn time you called." The old man coughed. "Damn cigarettes. I quit two years ago, haven't stopped hacking up a lung ever since."

He nodded as if his father could see him. "If you quit, how come you have a pack in the freezer?"

"In case of emergencies." The old man wheezed in a breath. "Enough with the pleasantries, what's going on there?"

"Ran into a bit of a snag here." Jake relayed the case developments to his father. "What the hell could be on that phone and flash drive?"

"This is crazier than a raccoon on meth." The old man paused. "Let me do some digging on this end. In the meantime, you play it cool."

"Will do." He paused, chewed his thumbnail and spit it out the window. "You eat today?"

"Little of this. Little of that. You know chemo can't kill my appetite."

Jake pictured the Francis Warrick of his youth. Tall. Strong. A Lucky Strike always dangling from his lip. Contrast that with the wisp of a figure he cut today. Damn. Cancer was a bitch. Lung cancer? The queen bitch.

"Glad to hear it."

"Don't need you to be glad. Need you to get this case in your rearview and get your ass back here. I can't do it all, you know."

"I know."

"Good. Now give Burlington a call. He wants a progress report."

"Will do. Bye."

"What, you're too big to tell your old man you love him?"

"No, sir" Jake grinned into the phone. Dad had been all huff and puff as long as he could remember. "Love you, Dad."

"Love you too." A cough rang through the phone. "Now get your ass back to work."

Jake hung up and flipped open the case file and found Burlington's personal cell number. What the hell could he tell him? No parent wanted to hear their daughter's killer spent his free time terrorizing other women. They had to be sick with grief. Jake wished he had better information to offer than he did.

He'd worked with Burlington before, the guy was a pain in the neck, but no one deserved this. He pictured Burlington in his corner office. Short and skinny with Mick Jagger hair, the hedge fund manager thought of himself as a master of the universe. The fact he hadn't saved his daughter must be agonizing.

Burlington answered on the first ring. "Good to hear from you, Mr. Warrick. I hope you have good news I can share with my wife."

"No, sir. But the sheriff's investigation is progressing."

"And the phone? Have you recovered it?"

Jake's trouble detector flared to life, raising goose bumps on his forearms. "No. Not yet."

"I understand that the woman who found poor Kendall is looking for the phone, too."

His body stilled but his heart jacked up to a hundred miles an hour. "How do you know that?"

"It doesn't matter. What *does* matter is that I get that phone. Also, Kendall had a flash drive. I want them both."

Burlington's superior tone and demands grated on Jake's self-control. This wasn't parental grief talking. "If I did find the phone and flash drive, I'd have to turn them over to the sheriff's office."

"Mr. Warrick," Burlington's voice turned icy. "You will do no such thing. The woman has what I want. She must. I do not care if you have to fuck her or frisk her to get them, but you *will* get them."

Jake snorted with disgust. "I'm not one of your so-called bodyguards, Burlington, who take care of the less savory aspects of your personal life. I won't break the law for you."

"How about for your father?"

His gut collapsed in on itself. "Who the hell do you think you are?"

"Who am I? I am the man who can guarantee your dying father lives long enough to see the company he built from scratch fall apart. Loans will be called in. Francis Warrick will be watching his business go belly up while hooked to a chemotherapy drip. Do you understand, Mr. Warrick?"

"You bastard." Jake ground the words out.

"Get me the phone and flash drive, or your father will face the consequences."

If Jake could reach through the phone, he would clamp his hands around Burlington's privileged throat. "I'll see you pay for this."

"I doubt it. I expect to hear from you soon, Mr. Warrick." Burlington disconnected.

Jake glared at his phone. Impotent fury blazed through him, locking his muscles and sending his blood pressure sky high.

The phone and flash drive had to be at Harvest, because they hadn't appeared in Kendall's dorm room, car or the Dumpster where Claire had found her. He'd talk Claire into searching again. Once they found them, he'd make the phone and flash drive disappear. She'd never have any idea it was him. He'd take the devices and hit the road.

Kendall's killer would still think Claire had the phone and flash drive. He'd come after her again.

The thought twisted Jake's insides, but he couldn't put the old man through Burlington's version of hell. Anyway, Hank would take care of Claire and catch the killer. He was just a private investigator. Her brother had the entire county sheriff's office behind him. She'd be fine.

Jake had to pick, and family came first. He was making the right decision.

So why did he feel like shit?

He hurled his phone out the SUV's open window. It shattered as soon as it hit the concrete parking lot.

"Hey man, you okay?" A pimply teenage boy wearing a red and blue King Pizza uniform stood outside the passenger-side door.

"Yeah, fine."

The boy gulped, his wide eyes aimed at the smashed phone. "Well, Benny said your pizza is ready. You can go in and get it if, uh, you're, uh, ready."

"Thanks." Jake rolled up the windows and stepped down from the SUV.

He didn't head to King Pizza. Instead, he dug his SIM card out of the pulverized mess in the parking lot and walked next door into the electronics store. A buy-one-get-one-free sign dominated the front window.

A few minutes later, two new cellphones in hand, he picked up the pizza, ready to drive back to Claire's. He slid the pizza box onto the passenger seat and tossed one of the phones into the glove compartment. The other phone sat charging beside him.

The twenty-minute drive went fast. Too fast. He spotted Claire's house as soon as he turned off the highway. Painted a virginal white with dark-green shutters, the house stood alone on the vast prairie. Jake flinched at the idea of sullying it with his presence.

"Damn." He slammed his palm down on the steering wheel as he pulled into Claire's driveway. "There's no other choice."

Onion trotted over to the SUV as soon as it stopped. Jake sat, frozen behind the wheel. Dread careened through his veins. It made his limbs heavy and created a dull ache in his chest.

He grabbed the pizza box, its warmth stealing into his palm. Onion panted beside him as he walked up to the porch. Jake's self-loathing grew with each step he took.

"Fuck." He couldn't do it.

There had to be another way. He'd find it, and Burlington would pay.

જાજાજા

The last nail pounded home with a satisfying thud. Claire stepped back and surveyed the plywood-covered front door. She pushed against its rough surface. It gave a little, but not too much. As a bonus, all that whacking had done wonders for her mood. She'd pictured the Voice of Doom's face on each nail. Smashing the hammer had been cheap therapy.

Still, as her temper relented, doubts about her decision to stay home raced through her mind. Really, did she want to be the delusional scream queen who thought she could take on a killer?

Big no to that one. She wanted to live to see the Voice of Doom rot in jail.

A quick set of taps on the door made Claire jump. She clutched the hammer, claw side out, arched high and ready strike.

Her body tensed. "Who is it?" The words came out in a high-pitched squeal.

"Pizza delivery."

Jake. Thank God. Unbidden, a nervous giggle escaped. She lowered the hammer to her side and opened the door.

Looked like her body wasn't the only one drawn to Jake. Onion sat by Jake's boot-clad feet. Great. Puppy love. Her stomach growled as she inhaled the scent of melted mozzarella and greasy pepperoni. Jake quirked an eyebrow.

"Come on in." Claire stepped back to let Jake inside. The dog followed behind, his ears perked up into perfect triangles. "*Et tu*, Brute?"

Onion's tongue lolled out of his mouth. Without even stopping to be petted, he followed the pizza scent into the house.

Jake, already in the kitchen, popped open two bottles and handed her one. The dark, porter-style beer slid down her parched throat like bitter honey. Heaven. Her body unwound all the way to her toes. She couldn't have been more relaxed if she was neck-deep in a vanilla bubble bath, a glass of Malbec wine balanced on the tub's edge and Chef Anthony Bourdain's latest book in her hands.

They ate in companionable silence, standing around the kitchen island. The setting sun filtered in through the window and acted as their candlelight. Onion wandered from one to the other, occasionally successful at begging a piece of pepperoni.

"So..." Claire watched the string of cheese connecting a pizza slice to Jake's delectable mouth. "Is this how your days normally go?"

He laughed and swiped at the wayward cheese. He swirled it around his finger and deposited it in his mouth. Claire's knees turned to jelly.

"No. Normally, I spend most of my time in the office working on computer investigations for businesses dealing with corporate spies. Every once in a while I'll spend the afternoon tailing a cheating spouse, but that's rare."

"Really? I kind of pictured you always up in someone's personal space."

"Nah, I prefer to let my brain do the work." He paused, looking Claire up and down. "But when it comes to play, I'm all about being in someone's...personal space."

Heat raced up from her toes. There was no missing the meaning behind that. The dinner's easygoing vibe dissolved into heated anticipation. Would it really be so bad to touch him? They were comrades in arms facing off against the Voice of Doom.

And man, it would be amazing to be wrapped up in his arms.

Claire licked an errant bit of sauce from the corner of her mouth. "So why are you here on a murder investigation?"

The leer slid off his face, blank affability taking its place. "It's the old story of money and power. Kendall's dad has plenty of both and uses them to ensure things turn out the way he wants. Like having me on this case. His company is our biggest client. We weren't going to turn him away when he asked for a favor." Jake polished off his second piece of pizza and reached for a third. "Now it's my turn. How'd you end up at Harvest?"

"Long story."

"I'll be here all night."

The idea made her insides whirl, picturing his tan legs twisted in her white silk sheets, the bed rocking beneath them. One bold move and she could make it happen. Contemplating, she nibbled on her crust then dipped one end in the marinara. "I grew up wanting to be a chef. As a kid, I had the hat, the white jacket, everything. But I cannot cook to save my life. I went to business school instead. After graduation, I managed a restaurant in Denver."

"How'd you end up back in Dry Creek?" He flicked a pepperoni slice to Onion. The dog snapped it out of midair.

Her stomach lurched at the thought of Brett. Handsome. Funny. Smart. Scumbag. They'd been together three years, lived together for two. She'd made him the center of her world, turned down job offers at restaurants in New York to stay close to him.

She'd found out how misplaced her trust in the shit had been when she'd discovered him in bed with another woman. She'd kicked him to the curb. In retaliation, he'd emptied their joint bank account and gotten engaged. The asshole probably used her last paycheck for the engagement ring. Pissed off all over again at the unfairness of fate, she took in a cleansing breath.

"Old story. Girl meets boy. Girl falls in love. Boy sleeps with another girl." She shrugged as if it didn't still hurt. "I came home, opened Harvest and here I am."

Jake had inched closer to her while she talked. Her hip touched his thigh. His body heat seeped in, scattering her thoughts.

"What's the idiot's name?"

"Brett Green, why?"

"That way I know who to slug if I ever meet him."

She laughed. Pounding Brett was a fantasy she nurtured herself. Jake reached for a napkin, his elbow grazing the side of her breast.

"How about you?" Her voice squeaked. Hoping to distract herself from his hard body, she swept the pizza crust crumbs scattered across the island into a small pile.

"No, I haven't fallen in love with a boy recently." He chuckled. "So, do killers tend to stalk you on a regular basis?"

She shrugged. "I'm just a boring restaurant owner. Half the time I think Harvest owns me, I'm there so much. No excitement in my life except when a customer's car gets towed."

"Too bad. You seem like a woman who enjoys stimulation."

Right now, she had too much stimulation, judging by the dampness between her legs. Desperate to put something in her mouth before she said something stupid, Claire reached for another slice of pizza but hesitated. Her hand hovered over the only piece left.

"We can arm wrestle for the last slice." Jake's voice warmed her skin as if he'd touched her.

Claire took in his thick biceps. Without thinking, she reached out toward him, but squashed the impulse. Memories of Brett had her on guard again. Jake was the definition of eye candy; pretty to look at, bad for her heart. Her hand switched course. She grabbed her beer and took a swig.

A mouthful of the dark liquid went down the wrong pipe. Coughing, she gasped for breath. Jake patted her back until she regained her normal breathing ability.

But his hand didn't move. It stayed between her shoulder blades, fingers spread wide. Sparks shot outward from his palm through her body.

Her breath slowed. Awareness prickled her skin. She yearned for his touch. Everywhere. Her lips parted. Slowly, she turned around. His hand left a trail of fire as it slid down and around her body until it landed on the curve of her hip.

He brought up his other hand to brush a stray hair from her face. His eyes drew her into his sexual orbit.

"You have some sauce right here." His voice's deep timbre sent an unmistakable signal to which her body responded. Her breasts became full and heavy. Her clit demanded attention.

He wiped the spot by the corner of her mouth with his thumb, then tracked the red liquid across her bottom lip. His head dipped lower. Hers moved up. When their lips met, thoughts of Brett and the Voice of Doom disappeared.

His firm tongue stroked her lips and begged for entry. She opened and his tongue swept in. She wrapped her tongue around his, dared him to taste his fill. The hand on her hip tightened and pulled her closer to his hard body. In return, her fingers found their way to the bottom of his T-shirt and started an upward exploration. His coarse chest hair tickled her palm, so alien and enticing at the same time.

His lips left hers and traced down her neck. He arrived at that sweet spot where her throat met her shoulder. Her spine dissolved as he sucked and nibbled.

"You taste so good," he said, his breath hot against her skin.

The feel of his hands cupping her ass made it impossible to respond verbally other than to moan her appreciation. Her body slid up against his as he lifted her to sit on the kitchen counter. He yanked her closer. The hard bulge in his jeans rubbed against her in the perfect spot.

Every part of her, relaxed only a few minutes before, hummed with tension. Her nipples stiffened into tight nubs. She squeezed her legs around Jake's waist, her wet core snug against him. She clutched at his shirt, desperate to touch his skin. She needed him closer. Her body demanded it. The endorphins wrapped around her brain gave the go ahead.

She hiked up his shirt and ran her hands up his strong back, felt the tension within him. He tugged her scoop-necked T-shirt lower and his lips descended to the top of her cleavage. He licked and kissed above her teal bra.

Claire's butt started to vibrate.

Not Jake making my ass vibrate.

It was her phone stuffed into her back pocket. She had to stop to answer. Her body screamed no.

"Phone," Claire panted. She pushed against Jake's shoulders. "Have...to...answer...my...phone."

He groaned into her breasts, put his hands on the counter on either side of her hips and lifted his head. The dark look in his eyes showed he hated this interruption as much as she did.

She got lost for a moment in those eyes. She wanted him. Now. Here on the counter. The vibration stopped but began again a second later. Jake swung her down so she stood again on the kitchen's taupe tile.

"You'd better answer that." He backed away, his desire palpable.

Claire reached into her back pocket, warm from Jake's touch, and pulled out the scarlet phone.

"Hello?" Her voice sounded breathy to her own ears.

"You know, I don't like to work this hard for the things I want. Do you understand what I'm telling you?"

Panic exploded in her stomach at the first syllable from the Voice of Doom. Claire looked up at Jake, who cocked his head in question.

"I understand. You want the phone and flash drive, but I don't have them. I looked everywhere."

Jake stepped closer. He leaned his head toward the phone. She angled it outward so he could listen.

"Your lack of results has, well... Sweetheart, I'm not the kind of guy you want angry." His voice pitched lower, sounding more like he did at the train tracks. "Lucky for me, I'm not angry. I. Am. Furious."

Claire's temper snapped. Again. This nutcase killed Kendall. He threatened her and her family. He trashed her house. And he had the gall to go all drama king on her for something she didn't have and couldn't find? She'd had enough.

"Welcome to the club, asshole, because I'm not too happy myself after the job you did on my house."

"Just wait, Kitten, you haven't seen anything yet." He hung up on her. Again.

Claire's fingers itched to throw the phone across the room, but her rational, penny-pinching side intervened. With deliberate care, she placed it on the counter.

"The guy is unhinged," Jake said.

"Yeah, I think the meth mind warp has set in. I'd give him the damn phone and flash drive if I had them. Why does he want them so badly?" Claire paced away from Jake, her bare feet slapping on the floor.

She stopped when Jake didn't respond. Intuition kicked in.

He knew something.

"What do you know?" Her gaze locked on him. He returned her look, but his face betrayed no emotion.

"Client confidentiality. I'd tell you if I could, but I can't."

She stalked across the kitchen to him.

"This guy is messing with my life." She jabbed her pointer finger into Jake's less-than-flexible pecs. "He wants the phone and flash drive enough to kill for them. If you know why, you'd better start talking. There are lives at stake!"

She stared up at his kiss-swollen lips. They stayed immobile. She counted to twenty, silently, and waited for a response. Jake remained quiet.

Claire took a step back. Outrage dominated, but underneath was a nugget of regret for what could have happened if the phone hadn't interrupted them.

"Get out."

"I'm not going anywhere. It's not safe for you to be alone." Jake took a step toward her, his hand outstretched. She shook her head and turned her back to him.

"So nice of you to care about my safety. Get out." Unwanted tears threatening to cascade down her cheeks, making her vision blurry.

"No." He turned her around to face him. His thumb brushed away an escaped tear.

Claire focused on his scuffed boots, pushed his hands away from her face. "Please, just leave," she said, her voice scratchy.

She stayed rooted as his footsteps receded from the kitchen. The front door's click announced Jake's departure. She blinked slowly and bit her lip. A part of her, one she didn't want to acknowledge, mourned.

Chapter Seven

I hope I never set eyes on Jake Warrick again." Claire flung a disinfectant wipe into the garbage. "Unless it's to hear him grovel at my feet."

Onion cocked his head at Claire and whined before trotting into the living room. No doubt he wanted to escape the heavy lemon scent filling the kitchen. She'd used so many wipes on the counters trying to wipe away the memory of those searing kisses, the room reeked of citrus.

The garbage disposal clanked as she fed it that fateful last slice of pepperoni pizza. She could have tossed it in the trash, but seeing it obliterated satisfied her more. She needed to see it get torn apart. It was a visual reminder of how her heart would have looked if she'd spent any more time in the secret-keeping snake's arms. Good riddance to the pizza and all other reminders of Jake.

But not the beer. That remained in the back of the fridge. Claire had her limits. She'd demolished a perfectly good slice of pizza, but it was just wrong to dump the beer. Especially when it was her favorite kind, Black Bart Porter. All other signs of Jake's visit had been removed.

Except for his SUV in her drive.

Peeking out the kitchen's crisp white curtains, she spied Jake sitting in his SUV. His muscular frame was outlined by the setting sun filtering in his windows. He'd never left.

Earlier, she'd marched outside, rapped on his rolled-up window and tried to shoo him off, but he wouldn't go. Told her she'd have to call Hank in to arrest him. Then he rolled up his window, leaned back in his seat and ignored her. She'd stomped back inside.

"Big jerk." She snapped the curtain shut.

Why had she ever kissed him? Hell, why did she still want to?

The shrill ring of her landline blasted the quiet. Claire eyed it warily. Not a lot of good things had resulted from phone calls lately. However, it went against her curious nature to let the phone go unanswered. She crossed to the counter in two steps and picked up the cordless receiver. She shot a quick glance at caller ID and smiled.

"Hey there, if it isn't Miss Beth Martinez, esquire. Done with work?" She had given her best friend the barest details before going to work on the front door earlier, promising they'd talk more once Beth got out of a client's deposition.

"Oh my God, what happened now? I just heard about how you chased down the killer. Margret Goodwin said she saw Chris carry you back to the restaurant. Are you okay?" Beth accentuated her words with a loud slurp of her ever-present coffee.

"I kissed him."

"You kissed the Voice of Doom?" Beth's voice went up three octaves.

"No, I did not kiss *him*! I kissed Jake. Well...more than that." Claire wandered into the living room and nudged Onion off the couch. "Not a lot more, but not as much as I wanted. We almost went at it right there on the kitchen counter. I can't seem to control myself around him."

She bent and picked up a few stray dog hairs from the overstuffed gray cushions. Onion shed fur everywhere and it seemed to travel with Claire. She'd found dog hair in her office at Harvest, where he'd never been, carried in on some item of her clothing.

"You really like him." Beth giggled. "Miss Picky Dater has finally found a guy who makes her melt."

"I don't know what you're talking about."

"Oh, come on, Claire. You've lived like a nun for long enough. There's nothing wrong with having the hots for Mr. Tall, Dark and Studly."

"Very funny. I don't live like a nun, I just work a lot. Anyway, it won't work out because we hate him."

"We do, huh?"

"Yep."

"More information, please."

Claire harrumphed and plopped down on the couch, still warm from Onion. "At Harvest, he questioned me like I was a criminal."

"So he did his job as a private investigator?"

Unable to sit still, Claire popped up from the couch and marched over to the bay window. Yep. He was still out there, his SUV bracketed by the storm clouds rolling across the pink and gold horizon.

"Beth, you're not helping. He's obnoxious. Plus, he knows why Kendall's phone and flash drive are so important, but he won't tell. Some bullshit about client confidentiality."

"As a lawyer, I must remind you that client confidentiality is not just 'some bullshit'."

"This is why everyone hates lawyers."

"Only until they need one. Enough lawyer jokes. Start talking, Claire."

She told Beth about Jake, the killer's latest phone call and her trashed house.

"I know you don't want to hear this, but it is not safe for you to stay out there by yourself."

"Agreed. So you're good with me coming to your place?"

"Of course! We'll watch a chick flick and talk shit about Jake. I have mocha coffee ice cream and whipped cream." Beth paused. "I'm on my way to get you now. Will you be okay until I get there?"

"Sure, I'm not alone. Jake's sitting in my driveway."

"What?"

"He wouldn't leave. Told me I'd have to get Hank to come arrest him."

Beth laughed so hard she snorted. "Oh my God, have you ever met your stubborn match." She sighed and took another loud slurp of coffee. "Okay, I'll be there in about twenty minutes."

"See ya then." Claire clicked the phone off. Her gaze locked on the SUV. Despite her irritation, having him out there set off the butterflies in her stomach again. Made her imagine what it would be like to have Jake around all the time.

Onion's nails clicked on the hardwood floor. He stopped in front of the plywood-covered front door and whined. She reigned in her fantasy and opened the door.

The dog lingered in the doorway and sniffed. Ozone hung heavy in the air. The wind whipped up low-lying dust devils. She snuck a look toward the SUV. Jake sat up straighter in his seat and watched her, intensely enough to spark goose bumps. She tore her gaze away, turned her face upward.

"Not looking good, Onion. You'd better pee now before Beth gets here."

The dog looked up with despondent eyes. Great. Her worry had spread to Onion.

"You moody dog. Get moving."

Despite her growing unease, Claire stepped out onto the porch. She figured Onion would come along too. Instead, his sorrowful eyes remained locked on the distance. He bayed an eerie howl.

"Okay, now you've freaked me out, Onion." She searched the fields for a sign of life, any hint that something or someone who didn't belong hid among the corn. She wished she had the shotgun in her hands instead of it being on the fireplace mantle.

The first fat drops of rain plopped against the ground. Claire didn't worry about the storm. The only good part of these fast-moving summer squalls was they tended to leave as quickly as they approached.

"Come on, let's go in until this blows over. Beth will be here soon. Don't worry."

She glanced toward the SUV. Jake gave her a quick salute. Pretending not to notice, she headed inside. If he'd fess up, she'd be more than happy to let him inside. But as things stood, he could enjoy the storm from his car.

Desperate to ignore the niggling apprehension, she focused on keeping her hands busy. The living room still needed work. She grabbed a well-worn copy of *Gone with the Wind*, and a hardcover copy of a Nina Simone biography to put back in the bookcase.

A crack of thunder broadcasted the storm's arrival. Nerves already frayed, Claire jumped. The books dropped from her grip. She looked over at Onion, who cowered under the coffee table.

Another crack of thunder. The house lights brightened, then flickered out. Onion, never one for storms, crawled out from his hiding spot to stand by Claire's side.

"It's okay, boy. Let's go flip the fuse." She fought to keep her voice calm. The sudden gloom strummed her already tightly strung nerves.

Claire felt her way along the walls to the fuse box in the back bedroom. She flipped the switches back and forth. No luck. Onion shivered at her feet.

"Flashlight and candles in the kitchen, come on." She scratched behind his ears, tried to impart a reassurance she didn't feel herself.

The storm turned the dusk sky to night. Claire tripped over the books piled on the floor on her way to the kitchen, but caught her balance before she landed face first. As soon as her foot crossed the kitchen threshold, another bolt of lightning lit up the sky. Claire caught a flash of something in the window over the kitchen sink.

She stifled a scream and instinctively stepped away from the window. Darkness blocked her vision of whatever, or whoever, had been there.

"Jake? Is that you?" Her shaky voice barely lifted over the sound of hail pinging against the roof.

Claire froze. No one answered. Dread filled her veins, chilled her skin.

The shotgun was in the living room. Should she go for it? A bang of thunder shook the windowpanes. She used her left hand to pull open the junk drawer and fumbled around for the flashlight.

Onion's throat vibrated as he let out a low growl. He stood, tense, by her side. At last, she felt the plastic tube. Her pulse ratcheted down a tad when she clutched the flashlight. With the push of a button, light poured forth toward the window.

Claire screamed at the face that glared at her. Only it wasn't the killer who stared back. The light showed her petrified reflection. She couldn't see who or what, if anything, was outside.

Never looking away from the window, she shuffled backward into the living room and grabbed the shotgun down from the mantle. She snatched up a box of shells and shoved them into a pocket. A few strays slipped out and plinked against the brick hearth. She loaded the gun by muscle memory, grateful for the times her dad had taken her hunting.

The flashlight didn't help make her feel safe. The gun helped, but....

She hunched low and scurried to the bay window. Lightning flashed. For a moment she saw Jake's SUV, too brief to confirm if he was in there. She scooted toward the door, the living room wall firm against her back—her goal, the front door and Jake beyond it.

Another burst of light. Onion stood growling at the kitchen door. The hair on his haunches stood straight up. The dog burst into wild, ferocious barking.

Claire swung the shotgun over. Pointed it at the kitchen door. "Who's there?" Her voice sounded stronger than she felt. No one responded.

Jake would have called out.

Her finger caressed the trigger.

If the Voice of Doom lurked outside, she couldn't afford to be a damsel in distress. She took in a steadying breath. Gritted her teeth. A calmness descended. No more fear. She knew what she had to do. She took in a deep breath and let it out. She was ready to fire at whoever came through the door.

Then...nothing.

Onion stopped barking, trotted across the kitchen and took several long, deep sniffs at the bottom of the door. He jogged back to Claire, his tail wagging.

"Good boy, Onion. Good boy."

She looked down at the shotgun in her white-knuckled hands. Unable to hold it any longer, she placed it on the fireplace's brick hearth. Her blood rushed through her body so fast, she could swear she heard the ocean.

Claire slumped against the wall and slid to the floor. She ran her trembling fingers through her hair. The rain beat down nearly in time with her hammering heart, but the thunder and hail had passed.

A rapping at the bay window startled her. She jerked her head up. Jake stood on the other side of the pane, his dark, rain-soaked hair plastered to his head. "Are you okay?"

His words, muffled by the window, shot straight to her heart, calmed its beating. Unable to form any words, she pushed up off the floor and crossed to the door. She tugged it open and cool air stroked her cheeks. The breeze brushed the hair off her shoulders.

Jake folded her into his arms. His chin rested on her head, a warm drop of rainwater sliding down one side of her face, a baptism of sorts. She'd acknowledged her fear. Asked for help. Received it. Found safe harbor. Wanted more.

"It's going to be okay." Jake stroked her hair. "I've got you."

And that's what scared her more than the storm—or the killer. She teetered on the edge of falling for a man she knew nothing about. After Brett, she'd worked hard to block access to her heart. Jake shook down her barriers like an earthquake.

He'd be gone as soon as they trapped Kendall's killer. She couldn't take another heartbreak. It had taken so long to come back from the last one.

"Claire—"

A car horn interrupted him. She peeked around his arm and saw Beth's Mini Cooper in the driveway.

"I have to go." She stepped away. Confusion was clear in his eyes and it gut checked her. Claire stood on her tiptoes, gave him a kiss on the cheek. "I can't do this. I'm sorry."

She trudged across the muddy drive with Onion at her heels, her tears camouflaged by the rain. If it hurt this bad to walk away, what would staying have been like?

Part of her wished she'd been brave enough to find out.

✎✎✎

Jake watched the tiny car drive away, Onion's head sticking out the passenger window. His solar plexus ached as if he'd been sucker-punched by a bear. He double-checked the latch on the front door and started toward his SUV.

Something slapping against a solid surface caught his attention. On alert, he stopped in his tracks and listened. There it was again.

Every nerve attuned to any movement, he grabbed the Beretta from his ankle holster. He crept toward the kitchen side of the wraparound porch. Turning the corner, he saw a hotel do-not-disturb sign hung from the kitchen doorknob.

Taking his time to be thorough, he scanned the perimeter. Spotting nothing out of the ordinary, he squatted down by the door. Scratches marred the lock. He picked the lock and cautiously entered Claire's kitchen. His search didn't turn up anything new and he returned to the porch and the do-not-disturb sign.

As he had done when he'd found the gas can in Claire's pantry, he used his cellphone camera to document the find. He e-mailed the latest photo to his Absolute Security account. Still alert, he got into his SUV and turned on his cellphone's hands-free option.

"Call Sherry."

It rang twice. "What's up, hot stuff? You finally callin' to ask me out on a date?"

"Oh honey, you know I would, but Carl would kill me if I took his blushing bride out on the town. You'd never be able to live with him afterward."

"Hell, I can't live with the man now. Do you know he brought home another stray dog today? We're up to five. Good Lord in heaven, it's a sin what I pay for dog food every week."

The news didn't surprise Jake. He'd grown up with Carl in the house next door and Sherry across the street. For as long as he'd known Carl, almost thirty years, he had been dragging home every pitiful animal he found.

"That's what you get for marrying a vet."

"True. So what's got you calling me if it's not candlelight dinners?"

"I need some help of the unofficial kind."

"Uh-huh. Talk."

He could tell by her no-nonsense tone he was now addressing Sgt. Sherry Newsome of the Denver Police Department.

"I've got an UNSUB believed to have killed a woman, now terrorizing another. I'll upload the case file to you as soon as I get to my hotel. I need to know if his pattern fits any open cases in Colorado, Nebraska or Wyoming."

"Shit, you're not asking for much, are you?"

"Do I ever?"

"Only every damn time. Are you working with the locals on this?"

"There's an evening at Silvio's in it for you and the puppy collector."

"Damn. You're gonna get me fired one of these days."

He shrugged. "Hey, what are friends for?"

"Technically, you're Carl's best friend, not mine. But I'll see what I can come up with."

"Thanks, Sherry, I owe you."

"Believe me, I keep a running tally."

Jake clicked off as he pulled onto the highway. The killer could have left the door hanger when he'd rummaged around the house. But if that was the case, why break the stained-glass front door?

Could the killer have been there during the storm? From his vantage point in the drive, Jake had kept visual contact of Claire through the windows but couldn't see the kitchen door.

It all came down to the phone and flash drive. What the fuck was Burlington hiding? Time to find out. He pushed the phone's voice-activation button.

"Call Burlington."

Chapter Eight

*B*eth lowered her sunglasses. "Well, looky who's waiting for you."

Claire spotted Jake and sank down in the passenger seat of Beth's Mini Cooper as they pulled into Harvest's nearly empty parking lot.

"Why won't he just go away?" She groaned at the sight of Jake lazing against his SUV's bumper. Dark aviator sunglasses covered his eyes, but his full lips were turned up in a smirk. He tipped his head their way. Claire's belly went gooey. Hell, the man's hard body wrapped up in tight blue jeans screamed "fuck me". Her fingers itched to drag his zipper down and slide the denim off his muscular legs, before doing exactly that.

She forced her gaze away from him and turned her mind from the fantasies he inspired. Concentrating on the asphalt at his feet, still bearing ugly black marks from the Jeep fire, helped slow the lust streaming through her body.

"I told him about your interlude with the shotgun during the storm." Beth examined her French manicure, studiously avoiding Claire's penetrating gaze.

Claire's jaw dropped. "What?"

"I saw him at the Stop and Sip this morning. He ordered a large black coffee and picked up the tab for my mocha. I think that was nice, don't you?" She looked up, her heart-shaped face plastered with false purity.

Claire glared at her best friend. Beth might be many things, but sweet and innocent were not two of them. "Spill."

Beth rolled her eyes. "Okay. Look, I know we," she made air quotes with her fingers, "hate him. But you really like this guy, even if you're not ready to say it out loud."

"I don't even know this guy!"

Beth shrugged her shoulders. "Sometimes love works like that."

"You're thinking about my love life?" Claire waved her hands in the air as she searched for a valid argument to change Beth's mind. "You know I do have more important things going on right now, like a psycho killer stalking me."

Claire hoped she sounded more convincing to Beth than she did to her own ears. Beth arched a thinly waxed brow.

Damn.

"Honey, there isn't a nutjob in the world who can take you down. You're way too smart and stubborn for that." Beth slung her arm around Claire's shoulders and squeezed. "But Jake could really help. I know you want to do it all on your own, but no one ever does it completely alone."

"I have you." Claire rested her head on Beth's shoulder.

"Yes, you do. But I'm a master of mental jujitsu." Beth raised her mocha toward Jake. "I think super-stud over there probably knows the other kind."

Claire contemplated Jake. Her body lusted after him and her dog trusted him. Beth probably was right. Maybe Jake was what she needed right now. A bodyguard with benefits.

Last night's storm seemed like years ago. The sense of home she'd experienced wrapped in his arms was just a gauzy dream. In the light of day, the idea of no-strings-attached sex with Jake seemed possible.

She ignored the doubts. She could protect herself. He'd be leaving soon so her heart was safe.

Of course, first he had to tell her the truth about the phone and the flash drive.

"What are you plotting?" Beth seemed to always know when she was going to let her impulses guide her, which she admitted happened way too frequently.

Claire flipped down the car's visor. "I don't know what you're talking about." Checking her reflection in the mirror, she reapplied her lipstick.

A casual affair. Better yet, one time only. With the way he threw her mind and body into turmoil, she couldn't be confident she could stay emotionally detached if it was more than once. She glanced at him. Anticipation sent a shiver down her spine.

Confident in her decision, she gave Beth a quick hug, grabbed her travel mug of coffee and stepped out of the car. Beth beeped her horn as she pulled onto Main Street.

Jake said nothing as she walked past. Fishing the keys out of her overloaded purse, she wondered if he'd ever open his mouth. She unlocked the door and turned to face him. His arms were folded across his chest, his legs outstretched and crossed at the unlaced ankles of his tan work boots. All he needed was a cowboy hat tipped down low over his face and he'd be the epitome of nonchalance.

Yeah, right.

She nailed him with a glare. "You coming in or not?"

He smiled in response and ambled forward. Her gut sank to her toes. This might not have been such a good idea. Who was she fooling? Was it too late to take back the invitation?

Flustered, she whipped around and ran smack into the door. The emerging bump on her forehead throbbed, but her pride hurt more.

"You have the worst luck." Jake's breath fluttered by her ear as he spoke.

Claire shivered. His body heat seeped through to her back.

He reached past her and pushed the door open. "Don't worry, I'll keep watch on the door."

Claire ignored him and strode into the darkened restaurant.

She loved the stillness of Harvest in the morning before the chef arrived, the food delivery guys dropped off their goods and the phone started ringing. This was her kingdom and she ruled it well. While many restaurants failed within the first twelve months, Harvest had netted a profit its first year. Not much of one, but it had been money in the bank.

On Mondays, Harvest stayed closed for business. Her routine dictated she'd spend the day buried in paperwork. Unlike other Monday mornings though, today she had a six-foot lightning rod of sexual energy zapping the calm.

"Well, if you're staying, you might as well come on up to the office." Claire added a little extra sway in her hips and ascended the staircase.

Jake admired the view as he followed Claire up the stairs. Damn. He needed to keep his thoughts on protecting her, but all he could think about was how much he wanted to touch her soft skin again.

She had on some sort of strappy dress that made a man fixate on the thin pieces of fabric on a woman's shoulders. Or maybe it just made Jake obsess about the bright-red material highlighting Claire's lightly freckled shoulders. The skirt swished as she climbed the stairs. Momentarily it clung to one side of her round ass before switching direction.

She stepped onto the landing and turned toward her office before he drank in his fill. Denied lust slammed into his gut and places lower as she disappeared into her office.

She was spunky and stubborn with a smart mouth, all wrapped up in a sexy package that he desperately craved. He wanted to bury himself deep inside her and feel her come around him. That vision in all its variations had kept him awake and hard most of the previous night.

"You okay?" Claire's voice knocked him back to the present. "You look like you're in pain. Headache? I have aspirin."

The reality of her put his lustful imaginings to shame. She stood in her office doorway with her arms crossed underneath her breasts. Her stance pushed those touchable tits together and upward. The sun's rays shining from her office windows outlined her toned legs through her dress.

Aspirin wasn't going to fix what ailed him.

"I'm good." He clenched and released his hands in a failed effort to get his blood rushing in a different direction. A bit bowlegged, he walked into Claire's office.

She sat down behind her desk and powered up her laptop. Jake looked around for a place to sit. She'd covered almost every horizontal surface with stacks of paper, management books and dirty coffee cups. He grabbed a pile of manila folders off a hot-pink plastic chair, gently placed them on the floor and sat down.

He had no idea what to do now. He never figured she'd actually let him inside the restaurant.

Claire cleared her throat. "Tell me about the phone and flash drive."

Well, that explained why she let him in.

Jake searched for the right words to start his story. The conversation with Burlington last night hadn't been pleasant, but it had been productive. He'd convinced the privileged prick he would cooperate, but demanded to know the story behind the phone and flash drive. Burlington had agreed.

Claire's chocolate-brown eyes didn't waver. "Tell me now or get the hell out."

He scooted his chair closer to her desk and lowered his voice to a confidential tone. "Charles Burlington, Kendall's dad, adopted her when he and Kendall's mom, Charlotte, got married. Kendall was two years old at the time."

He leaned forward in his chair, swiped her coffee and took a long drink. Like him, she drank it black. He paid no mind to her irritated look as he returned the travel mug to her desk.

"It seems Kendall's biological father, Frank Darcy, is a two-time loser, con man and meth abuser who'd made contact with her earlier this year. He'd talked Kendall into giving him money—a lot of money. Burlington thinks Darcy killed Kendall."

"Why would Darcy kill Kendall?"

"Burlington believes Kendall stored the account information needed to access her money on the flash drive. Either she changed her mind about giving the cash to Darcy or his meth paranoia took over and he killed her for reasons that only make sense to him."

"No doubt the Voice of Doom was tweaking hard yesterday. Could it have been Darcy? He's in the right age bracket and he's definitely a meth head."

"Maybe. Burlington couldn't give me a good description of him, said he hadn't ever seen him and it had been years since the wife had. My office is searching arrest records now to pull a photo."

"Something still seems off." A worry line formed between Claire's eyes. "If she was giving him money already, killing her doesn't make sense, even for a meth addict."

"Agreed. Burlington did bring up a third possibility. Kendall siphoned off three million dollars from her parents to give to Darcy. Burlington thinks she did so at Darcy's request and that he killed Kendall to cover his tracks."

"How did Burlington find out about all this?"

"Kendall told her mother everything the day before she was killed."

She pursed her lips and squinted at him. "Why is my bullshit meter going crazy right now?"

"Because you're not a moron." He stole another drink of coffee. "Also, it's the second story he's told about why he wants the phone. The first story was his wife wanted some photos of herself and Kendall that were on the phone. Both stories are crap. Maybe not all of the embezzled money story is crap, but a good portion of it is."

He stood up, shoved his fingers through his hair. "Burlington is an asshole, but he's not stupid. I doubt anyone could siphon off twenty bucks from him, let alone three million. Something else is going on here. I don't know what Kendall stumbled onto, but it was enough to get her killed."

He lowered himself to the chair and stretched his legs out. "I did some research last night at the hotel, called up some buddies who owe me favors. There are questions about the legitimacy of some of Burlington's clients' profits. Maybe the three million dollars Kendall stole, if she took any money at all, didn't belong to her parents. Maybe it belonged to one of daddy's clients."

Jake gave Claire a moment to digest the information.

"Shit." The vivacious spark that usually glimmered in her eyes dimmed. "So how do we nail the son of a bitch who killed Kendall?"

God, he loved the spit and vinegar in her. She refused to give up. As a double bonus, she'd said "we".

"Same plan as before. We wait for him to come at you again, but this time I'll be with you."

She gave him a wan smile. Her obvious worry hurt him as if he'd been kicked in the knee. To lighten the mood, he leveled his best wolfish leer at her. "Enough of this. I'd rather talk about when we're going to finish what we started in your kitchen."

Claire pursed her lips and turned toward her screen. "We're finished with that." Her fingers sped across her keyboard.

He doubted anyone but an android from the science fiction channel could type that fast. Jake got up, circled the desk and stopped directly behind Claire's high-back office chair. The screen showed a mass of gibberish. Her shoulders tensed, but she didn't turn to look at him. He leaned down.

"That may be true, but I'm still not going anywhere." He twirled a strand of auburn hair, which had escaped from her loose bun. "I'm going to get the son of a bitch who hurt you."

She grasped his hair-wrapped finger. He expected her to pull her hair away, but she didn't.

"Is that the only reason you're staying?"

Her breathy question made his nuts tighten. "It should be." His concrete dick clearly didn't agree. "But right now it's not."

He brushed his lips against the spot below her earlobe. She smelled of oranges and crisp snowfall at the same time, a sensual contradiction much like the woman herself. He meant to stop there, but couldn't. He sucked on her earlobe, then nibbled down her neck and strung kisses across her shoulders.

"Jake," Claire half moaned, half whispered as she stood up and turned to face him.

Their mouths melded together. His hands traveled up the outside of her smooth thighs and lifted her dress. He caressed her ass before he lifted her up so she could wrap her legs around his waist. His hands on her butt locked her against his straining cock. She fit against him perfectly; it felt better than anything he'd ever experienced.

"Clarabell Anne Layton, you should count yourself lucky I'm not that so-called Voice of Doom Chris told me is after you. My Lord, here you are getting frisky."

The shrill voice shocked his hands still.

Jake's head shot up. A tall, middle-aged woman with fire-engine-red hair stood in the doorway with her hands on her hips. Bedazzled bull horns decorated her white T-shirt right above the words: Don't mess with Texas...or me.

"I could've shot you dead before you'd even gotten your lips off that man." She pressed her hand to her heart in a melodramatic fashion. "I failed as a mother. My child has no survival instinct." She lowered her neon-yellow sunglasses to the upturned end of her nose. Her hostile gaze burned a hole through Jake. "And as for you, Mr. Hands-On-My-Baby's-Behind, you'd better put my daughter down. Now."

He did as told.

ঙচঙচ

"Hi, Mom." Claire bit her kiss-swollen bottom lip. "You made great time from Texas."

Embarrassed heat burned from her toes to her ears as she looked at Glenda Layton. Of all the people to walk in on her and Jake, only the killer would have been worse.

"Mmm-hmm. Don't you try to give me the business. I know all about what's going on. Is this fella here to help protect your body or just molest it?"

"Mother!"

Jake's hand rubbed the small of her back. The caress comforted her, lessening the mortification swamping her.

"Now, if I was your age and hadn't met your dear father yet, I might agree to that second part myself." Glenda gave Jake the once over. "He is cute, isn't he?"

"This..." She waved her hands in the air. "This is just a fluke. It won't be happening again."

Jake stopped his hand's calming circle, and slid it south. He squeezed her butt. Desire swept through her like a brushfire. She planted one of her heels onto Jake's toes and ignored his strangled grunt.

Glenda had a small canary-yellow duffel bag on the floor next to her Keds. Claire lowered herself into her chair, her head aching.

"Mom, why do you have your overnight bag?" Unease crept up her spine. *Please say it's presents from Texas.*

"I'm coming to stay with you, of course. I'll be right next to you every moment of the day and night until Hank catches that murderer. Don't you worry. Nobody messes with the Laytons. We conquer, we don't cower."

Claire loved her mother, but there was no way she could move in. The last time her mother spent the weekend, she came home to find her kitchen rearranged, her voicemails deleted and her calendar filled with blind dates. That could not happen again.

"No need for you to do that, Mrs. Layton. I'm watching out for Claire until all of this blows over."

Claire flashed Jake a grateful smile. He winked in return.

"You that man from the security company who has Hank fit to be tied?" Glenda squared her jaw.

"Yes, ma'am, I guess so." He walked around the desk and offered his hand.

She shook it and held on. "Are you married?"

"No, ma'am." Jake shook his head.

"Girlfriend?"

"Not a one."

Glenda leaned forward. "Gay?"

As usual, her mom had her contemplating moving to Siberia. She couldn't be more humiliated if she had to run naked down Main Street during the annual Oh, Pioneer Parade.

"Nope." He grinned down at Glenda. It looked as if he had this conversation with every mother he met.

"Do you want to be married?"

She grimaced at the hopeful look on her mom's face.

"Not really."

"Why not?" Glenda dropped his hand and crossed her arms in front of her.

Jake shrugged. "Well, ma'am, I'm just not the marrying kind."

"We'll see about that." Excited speculation lit up Glenda's face. She dug into her makeup counter giveaway purse and brought out a polka-dotted notepad and pen set. She scribbled something and handed it to Jake.

"You call me if you need my help. I belong to the NRA." She turned her attention to Claire. "He goes, I stay. Got it?"

She mentally conceded the battle. With her mother, it always ended the same. "Yes, Mom."

"Good. Toodles."

She watched in silence as her mother stalked from the room. Groaning, she cradled her head in her hands.

"Wow." Jake's voice was tinged with awe.

"Yeah. My mother is...something else."

Claire glanced at Jake. He looked dazed, the normal reaction after meeting her mother, which was why she'd had only first dates in high school.

"Thanks for helping me. Telling her you were staying with me was brilliant. I appreciate it."

He leveled the full force of his slate-blue eyes at her. "I *am* staying with you."

"Oh no." Claire slapped her palms down on her desk. "That was just to get Mom out of here. There's no way you're staying with me."

She couldn't play house with him. Going to sleep listening to him breathe. Having coffee together in the morning. Brushing their teeth together in the bathroom. No way could she keep her heart in check in that situation.

In two long steps, he was beside her. He tugged at her elbow and spun her around to face him. "I won't let anything happen to you. You're safe with me."

He promised protection, but that wasn't what she wanted most from him. Maybe having her life turned upside down by a crazy man had bent her thinking. Perhaps she would have reacted this strongly to Jake under any circumstances. No matter the reason, she wanted this man, and wanted him badly.

"Am I?" Her gaze aimed for the erection visible through his jeans.

"Yes. I'm here for a job. That's all." A vein throbbed at his temple. "I don't want to want you, but I can't seem to help it."

What did she gain from denying herself the pleasure of him in bed as long as he didn't stay the night? Nothing. Her decision made, Claire embraced the sexual fever burning through her body, grabbed his waistband and pulled him close. "Is wanting me so bad?"

"Yes."

"Why?" She rubbed the bulge in his jeans and squeezed him lightly.

He grabbed her wrist, stopping her caress. "When this is over, I'm gone. My life is in Denver. Yours is here."

"True. But this is just lust, nothing more. Maybe once is all we need." She popped open the buttons on his jeans.

He sucked in a breath. "One time, no strings?"

Claire slid his zipper down. "Not unless you're interested in being tied up."

Chapter Nine

*C*laire freed Jake's straining cock from the confines of his cotton boxers. Her mouth watered at the sight of him, hard and thick. Heat swamped her body and the tingling sensation in her clit grew more ferocious. Her heart raced as she surrendered to the heady lust and banished any rational thought from her mind.

She wrapped her long fingers around him, but couldn't circle his girth completely. With deliberate care, she slowly slid her grasp up his silken flesh, and squeezed him when she reached the tight black curls at the base.

"Oh my God, Claire." His words ended in a low groan.

The sound sent a shiver of pleasure dancing up her spine. She sank to her knees and his warm dick pulsed in her small hands. Only inches from the bulbous tip, she opened her mouth. He drew in a sharp breath.

Claire hesitated, overcome by the depth of her desire. Pre-cum glistened on the smooth head, begging to be licked off. She licked her lips in anticipation, imagined sucking his dick into her mouth. She would stroke its tender underside with her tongue while cupping his tight balls. But she couldn't, not yet anyway. Tempering the urge to swallow him took all of her willpower, but she need to go slow and make the moment last.

She blew softly on his erection.

Jake shivered and arched his back. "God, Claire."

She ran her thumb across the clear droplets pooling on the head. Looking up at him, she brought her thumb to her mouth and licked the delicious taste of him off her skin. Like a cat with cream, she used the tip of her tongue to devour every drop of the salty liquid. She stared up at him, capturing his gaze as she relished his taste. His blue eyes smoldered and he entwined his fingers into her loosely bound hair.

"Damn." Jake tilted his head back and urged her mouth forward.

Her pussy began to throb to an ancient beat as her nipples tightened. Her raging libido heated her skin, making her breasts heavy and demanding she take him now. But she ignored the call. She planned to pack a lot into this single encounter.

Mesmerized by the beauty of him, she rubbed his delicate hardness up and down in tantalizingly slow strokes. Jake groaned and rocked his hips back and forth. The contrast of her cherry-red nails against his flushed dick made her so wet she soaked her thong.

"You have to stop or I'm going to come all over your hand." Sweet torment had tightened his square jaw. He let her go and curled his hands into tight fists at his side. His balls were pulled up tight.

They might only have this time together, but Claire planned to enjoy it to the fullest. She stopped the motion, but didn't remove her hand. "Not yet, you're not. We're going to make this one time only count."

After one last leisurely upward stroke and another body-shaking moan from Jake, she released his hard-on and reached up to his shirt. She tugged the crisp cotton from his waistband. The devil in her loved tormenting him with a slow strip down. She flashed him a saucy grin and sucked on her bottom lip as she rose to her feet.

Starting at the bottom, she unbuttoned his white dress shirt. Each inch of sinewy muscle sent her heart racing. Reveling in the beauty of his tan chest, she bent and placed light kisses on his freshly bared flesh. Tracing her tongue along the shadows of his abs, she savored the clean, soapy flavor. His slid his hands through her hair urged her to speed up, seconded by his heated moans, but Claire took her own sweet time. She'd never imagined unbuttoning a shirt could be so rewarding.

Once she'd dispatched the buttons, she slid her hands across his hard chest and pushed the shirt open. Claire's knees melted at the sight of his powerfully built chest. Her mouth went dry and she nearly lost her nerve. But her pussy clenched, and a tension started to build deep within her. Her fingers trailed across his hard abs, the tips tickled by his coarse hair. His muscles tightened under her touch. Traveling lower, she drew her fingers across a small scar.

"Appendix." His low growl sent her pulse rocketing.

She traced it with the tip of her nail.

He flinched. "That tickles."

A smile played on her lips as both hands, fingers spread wide, slid up his chest, parting the dusting of hair covering his torso.

"You...are...gorgeous." She meant it. Apollo would be jealous of Jake's form. He was the most beautiful man she'd ever seen.

Leaning forward, she lapped at his right nipple. It puckered and she closed her lips around the tight nub. She flicked it with her tongue. His resulting moan echoed her building excitement. Her clit twitched in anticipation of his touch.

He drew her upward, away from her prize, until she stood up straight. Misery and ecstasy warred on his face. On hers too, she imagined.

"Please." He ground out that one word.

She reached for the straps of her sundress and stepped out of his grasp. "Please what?"

Expressions flashed across his face as she slid first one strap, then the other off her shoulders. Lust, excitement, anticipation, hunger, they were all there. Usually she didn't vamp it up quite this much, but the idea of only getting one chance with Jake made her want to wring every bit of fun and passion out of the experience.

Her dress caught on her extended nipples. The soft cotton caress stoked her heat. A light tug freed the red dress. It skimmed over her hips on its way to the floor, where it lay in a pile around her feet. The heels on her brown leather sandals pushed her bottom out just so, an effect she took full advantage of as she teased and turned in a circle.

Jake reached out for her, but she evaded him. She raised her arms, pulled out the pins holding her hair in a bun and shook it out. The smooth tresses caressed her shoulders and upper back.

"Claire, please." His words sounded pained, but he looked as if he'd just opened up the world's best present.

He stood in front of her, shirt open and cock out but still dressed. Just when she thought she couldn't get any hotter, he took hold of his dick and watched her as he stroked.

Claire blew him a kiss and hooked her fingers into the band of her lacy, green thong.

"Enough." Jake grabbed her hips.

Propping her butt against the warm wood, Jake dragged her thong down and followed it to the floor. On his knees, he spread her legs, palms flat against her inner thighs. Anticipation strung her muscles tight. Her fingers tightened on the desk's edge as he leaned his face forward into her damp pussy.

But no tongue made contact, no fingers penetrated.

Surprised and frustrated, she looked down. Jake's slate-blue eyes met her gaze.

"Any plans to move to Denver?"

He picks this moment to get chatty? She wanted to scream. Her pussy ached for his touch to relieve the escalating tension inside her.

She shook her head. "No."

"Damn." He kissed her inner thigh.

His lips sizzled against her sensitive skin. Her whole body trembled.

He laid his head above her knee, wet a finger in his mouth then slid it home inside Claire. Her back arched at his welcome invasion. Pleasure rippled upward. He added a second and twisted them around, flicked against her G-spot. Claire's body went taut. She threw back her head, ground her core against the flat of his palm.

"I can't relocate here." His head inched closer to the exact spot where she wanted it, so close his words brushed against her tender flesh.

Awash in sensation, it took all of her mental powers to utter a single word. "No."

"Damn." He muttered the curse into her wet center, glided his tongue along her inner lips and circled her clit. A current of sexual electricity shot through her, making the rest of the world disappear.

"Yes." Claire didn't recognize the sound of her own hoarse voice strangled with desire.

His fingers slid in and out, stretched her open while his tongue continued its dance. Millimeter by millimeter his flat tongue slid up her wet lips. He stopped at her clit, sucked the nub into his warm mouth. His fingers thrust rhythmically against the bundle of nerves inside her vagina. She gasped as fire shot through her.

Hot waves rippled up from her pussy. They started slow, but increased in intensity and speed. Every part of her strained toward orgasm. Close. She was so close. His thumb pressed just below her sensitive button as he licked. She clutched his head, pushed him deeper. Her body constricted and she came undone.

"Jake!"

It took a few moments before she could uncurl her toes. When she could, she arched her back in a lazy, catlike stretch.

ప్రాలు ప్రాలు

The sight of her stopped Jake cold. Propped up on her desk, her skin glowing in the soft midmorning light. Dust particles danced around her like fairies protecting their sated queen. And here he was on his knees in worship.

Fairies? A queen? He was a hockey-and-beer guy, where the hell had fairy queens come from? Chagrined, he shook his head. "Damn, how did you do this to me?"

"Do what?" Her husky voice purred, thick with satisfaction.

"Make me want to keep you like this all the time."

She glanced down at her pleasured body. Her lips curled into a grin. "I might get cold come September."

He ran his hands up her smooth legs as he continued to kneel on the floor. Despite her short stature, they seemed to go on forever. The perfect size to wrap around his waist. His palms rested on her knees. He ran his thumb across a tiny patch of hair on her kneecap she must have missed when shaving. The short hairs pricked him. Damn. Even that turned him on.

He had to tell her about Burlington's attempt to blackmail him. He'd left that part out earlier, figuring what she didn't know wouldn't hurt her. But the lingering suspicion evident on her face had told him she'd known he'd been holding back.

When it came out in the open that he'd almost used her to find the phone and flash drive, she'd be pissed. After he told her he had planned to leave her to face off against the killer by herself, she'd be irate. And rightly so. But if he didn't tell her and she found out another way, she'd never forgive him. Jake couldn't live with that.

"Hey." Her fingers pushed his chin upward, her expression quizzical. "I didn't mean to scare you off with the September comment. I know this isn't long term. It's just a little fun. No harm. No foul."

Her body language belied her words. Shoulders hunched, she looked as if she awaited an emotional kick to the stomach. Her downcast eyes were half hidden behind a curtain of auburn hair. Her lip trembled for a moment before she tugged on it with her teeth.

Whoever that idiot Brett guy was, he'd pulled a number on Claire. Jake could tell she expected him to get up and go. Fuck that. This may not be forever, but while he had her, she was all his. And his Claire had too much spark to look so forlorn.

Rising up from the floor, he cupped her face in his hands, forcing her to read the truth in his eyes. "You can't get rid of me that easily."

He meant for the kiss to be soft and reassuring. But as soon as his lips brushed hers, he realized that wasn't going to happen. Instinct hardwired by centuries of evolution overwhelmed him. It demanded he claim this woman, make her his. Their tongues tangled as he melded her soft curves to his hard frame.

Claire pushed at his chest, forcing them apart. "Sit back in that chair. I want to be on top."

It killed him to deny her, but they couldn't do this until she knew the truth. "We have to talk."

Her palm settled on his stomach. "Why?"

"I have to tell you something."

She wouldn't look up at him. "It can wait."

"No, it can't." Mimicking her move from earlier, he drew her chin upward. "Burlington wants me to use you to find the phone and flash drive."

She jerked away from his touch. His body cooled in an instant. Hands on her hips, she stood with her feet shoulder-width apart. Her come-hither glance had been replaced with a drop-dead glare. Temper rolled off her naked body. Her face gave away everything, including a hint of hurt hiding behind the grim line of her mouth.

"And just how are you supposed to do that?" She practically spat the words at him.

Forget the fairy queen. His Claire was the world's shortest Amazon warrior. She amazed him. Scared him a little, too.

"Claire..." The answer stuck in his throat.

"What did he say?"

His body tensed. "Fuck you or frisk you." Just saying the words made his skin crawl. Seeing the resulting pain etched on her face was more than he could take. "Claire—"

"So that's what this was?" She flung her arms outward over her clothes piled up on the floor.

A puck to the head wouldn't have hurt as much as her accusation. "No!" She had to believe him. "I couldn't do it."

She stalked over to him. "What's wrong? Did it offend your delicate sensibilities to fuck on orders?"

"Claire, I knew I couldn't do it before I even got back to your house with the pizza yesterday." His gut churned at the thought of never touching her again.

"Why should I believe you?" Her stance remained aggressive, but her posture relaxed a few millimeters.

Jake slumped down into the chair that a few minutes earlier could've been the site of lovemaking bliss. Not now. He rubbed his hands across his face. If he couldn't make her understand, she'd be out of his life faster than a Bobby Hull slapshot. He'd rather be hit in the face by that shot than lose her now.

How the fuck had that happened?

"My father has stage four lung cancer. He's fighting it tooth and nail, but the fact is, he's dying." He drew in a shaky breath. "Burlington swore he'd make the old man's last few months a living hell if I didn't cooperate. But I won't sacrifice you for him. That's not the kind of man he raised me to be."

She regarded him silently, doubt still evident on her face. He grasped her hands in his, a now familiar electric current jolting him.

"There's something between us, Claire. I don't know what it is and I don't know how long it'll last, but I can't deny it. I will find a way to protect you *and* the old man."

She slid her hands out of his. "If you're lying to me, I'll make sure you live to regret it."

He pulled her down to his lap, tension migrating from his chest farther south, to where her naked ass snuggled up against his crotch. "I'd expect nothing less."

੭੦੭੦੭੦

The kiss's intensity seared Claire's lips. Her heart had already bought Jake's explanation. Her head, on the other hand, stayed suspicious.

Brett had been good at spinning tales, too. The late-night calls were about business. The perfume that clung to his jacket had been from a friend who'd sprayed his coat in jest. How many times had he told her it was all in her head? Too many to count.

Jake's arms tightened around her, bringing her back to the present. She broke the kiss. He wouldn't hurt her. She didn't have any proof. She didn't understand how she could be so sure, but she was.

Together they'd find a way to make Burlington pay and trap the killer, but not right now. She had plans for the growing bulge in his jeans.

"You have too many clothes on."

"I was thinking the same thing."

She jumped off his lap and hopped up on the desk to enjoy the show. Anticipation tickled her skin. His fingers paused at his waistband. She sucked on her bottom lip, her gaze glued to the action.

"Um, I don't suppose you have a condom?"

That drew her attention upward to his face. Claire mentally slapped herself. "No, but the Stop and Sip is around the corner."

She looked around for her clothes. Now, where did her thong go? *Why is it a girl can never find underwear at a time like this?*

Jake held up the swath of green fabric and twirled it around on his finger like a Hula-Hoop.

"Very funny." Claire yanked it from him. "Come on, we need to get there before the lunch rush. The last thing I need is Mary Beth Schneider to tell the whole town you and I bought condoms at the Stop and Sip."

She slipped into her underwear and shimmied her dress back on. By the time she was finished, Jake had already buttoned his shirt and zipped his pants.

She hated to see that get put away.

"You really should at least come visit me in Denver. I could take you to a hockey game."

Claire considered the situation. Funny, smart and hot as hell, Jake could make a girl delve into a long-distance relationship. An idea of life with him wormed its way into her thoughts. Hot sex. Cute kids. Growing old together.

But reality bitch-slapped the fantasy. He'd be gone soon. One night only. That was all her heart could take.

"No."

"Damn."

Quiet enveloped the room. Jake's lips pressed together to form a hard, straight line. Claire couldn't help herself; she lifted herself onto her tiptoes and softly kissed him.

"Damn."

"Will you stop saying that!" Claire slugged him in the shoulder and grabbed her purse. "Come on, we need to get moving."

She pushed back all thoughts of a future with Jake as they hurried down the stairs. Eagerness propelled her down the stairs. She couldn't wait to buy the condoms and take him home. What she wanted to do would take time and privacy.

"Come down for a bite before round two?"

Claire started. Her whole body tensed at the nasal tone—the same one she heard in her nightmares.

The Voice of Doom leaned against the back door. A lecherous gleam lit his eyes. He aimed a black handgun at them.

"Oh, don't get shy on me now, Red. I'd just love to hear all the details."

Chapter Ten

*H*is nerves taut, Jake took in the details of the situation. The stairs were at their backs. The dining room was in front of them. The gunman blocked the closest exit. It was the same nutjob from the Jeep fire, who'd been threatening Claire and had more than likely killed Kendall. He'd changed his clothes and shaved his head, but Jake couldn't mistake him or his malicious intent. Not with a 9mm Browning trained on Claire's heart.

"That was some scream." The killer lifted his glassy-eyed gaze toward Jake, but kept the gun pointed at Claire. "You'll have to share your secret with me after this is over. I can make the girls yell, but it's never my name."

Claire shook at his side. His protective urge stoked the fury rushing through his veins. That bastard would pay for making her life hell. The tweaker had some drug-powered aggression on his side, but Jake had no doubt he'd take the killer down. He hunched his shoulders like a lineman about to make a tackle and prepared to take out the lunatic.

The gun's ominous click stopped him cold.

"Loverboy, I've got no beef with you." He stepped closer to Claire, his movements jerky. "But if pushed, I'll kill you both."

Jake ground his teeth, his fists tight by his thighs. He wanted to howl in frustration. They'd wanted the killer to appear on her doorstep. But he'd let his dick and her sweet body distract him from the real reason he was here. To protect Claire. Now they were at this asshole's mercy instead of it being the other way around. He'd been a damn fool.

He grabbed Claire's forearm and tried to pull her behind him to shield her from the maniac. But she wouldn't go. Short of picking her up and moving her, there was no way to force her to the rear. He couldn't risk the killer panicking if he made that kind of move.

She took a step toward the gunman. Terror like he'd never known before gripped his spine. He moved in her direction, ready to do whatever it took to defend her.

"I have the phone and flash drive."

Her quiet words made him freeze in his tracks. His heart stopped for a moment. Could she have been lying all along? Was she involved more than he knew? Doubt nibbled away at him.

She stood halfway between his arms and the killer's gun. The hostess stand was just beyond her grasp. He spotted the tell-tale wet glisten on her cheeks. He refused to believe she'd lied to him. Not his Claire.

"I found them this morning in the bar when Jake brought up a new keg from storage." She reached the polished hostess stand and casually leaned on it with one hand.

Tension seeped from his body. Jake fought to keep the ah-ha look off his face. There was no keg this morning. Except for the slight tremble of her hands, he'd be hard-pressed to see through her story if he hadn't been here himself.

Her gaze stayed trained on the killer's face and no stutter gave her away. Most people panicked at the business end of a handgun, and for good reason. But not Claire. She'd come up with a plan to buy time. What a woman.

"Well, goodie." The man took a step forward, sweat beading on his upper lip, a tic making his right hand twitch as it held the gun. "Let's go get them."

She cast her head down and looked at him demurely through her lashes.

"How about a beer or a coffee while you wait?" She spoke the words as if the psycho had arrived early for a reservation. Obviously, Claire had chosen the role of good cop. No problem. The idea of taking a few phonebooks or rubber batons to this creep appealed to the dark place in Jake's soul, especially after all the asshole had put her through.

"Tempting as that offer is, I'm going to turn it down considering I don't want to leave fingerprints and all. Now get moving, Sweetcheeks."

Jake's fingers itched to wrap around this guy's throat, but the tweaker had the 9mm too close to Claire. He couldn't risk it. The killer waved the gun in the bar's direction.

She walked across the dining room until she was within Jake's grasp. He reached out and squeezed her hand. Holding her delicate hand in his reminded him how high the stakes were. In that moment, a calm certainty settled on him. He'd take a bullet for her, whatever it took to keep her safe.

Her steps seemed confident, but he spotted her worrying her bottom lip. He had to get the upper hand. Soon. They couldn't delay much longer.

A few distracted seconds, that's all he needed. This guy was sloppy. He guarded Jake in a perfunctory manner, as if it was all for show. Did he have backup hidden away? Jake didn't get that vibe and hadn't spotted anyone else, but he couldn't be sure. It wouldn't take much to get a drop on the killer, but if he failed, Claire would pay the price. That couldn't happen.

She rambled about the restaurant's history all the way to the barroom. Grace under pressure is what the old man would call it.

"We found this bar at auction in Cheyenne. Rumor has it Wild Bill Hickok sat at this bar in his Pony Express days." She stopped at the same spot in front of the wooden bar where she'd stood when they'd met. Right next to the water hose she'd sprayed him down with. "He might have had a shot of water, or something stronger, bellied up to this very bar."

God love her, she had come up with the perfect diversion. It just might work. He tried to relax his muscles. If the killer saw Jake was tense and ready to make a move, Claire's plan wouldn't work. A forced calm washed over him as he waited for just the right moment to attack.

"Fascinating. Really. I could sit her for hours forgetting about what I came here for. What was it now?" the psycho sneered. "Oh yeah, the phone and flash drive."

"They're behind the bar." She punctuated her quiet voice by waving toward the wood counter.

"Then go get them, Toots."

She gave Jake's hand another squeeze and walked behind the bar. He followed, wanting to keep his body between her and the gun barrel.

"Oh no." The killer jerked the gun around toward him. "I don't trust you either. You stay here by me at the end of the bar and you, Sweetheart, go get my stuff."

Jake's hands curled into fists. Dependent on what she would do next, he chomped at the bit to make his move. No matter how much he hated the fact, it was too early. He only had one shot at this. He had to wait for the perfect moment. Each second crawled by as she continued toward the keg at the far end of the bar.

"My brothers say I always talk when I'm nervous. I always thought they were full of it, but looks like they're right." Claire waved her hands in the air as she spoke and knocked the water hose from its perch. "Clumsy too. Damn. Can't you point that gun somewhere else? It's really putting me on edge."

"It's supposed to, Baby Doll."

She clutched the hose as if to replace it on the handle. Instead, she whipped the spout toward the gunman and let the water rip.

The shot caught him right in the mouth. Startled, his head snapped back.

"She's got wicked aim with that hose," Jake snarled as he smashed the killer's gun hand onto the bar. He let out a satisfying grunt, but hung on to the gun.

Determined to take the asshole out, Jake landed a solid elbow to the nose. The man screamed and dropped the gun on the bar with a thunk. It spun on the slick surface and fell to the floor.

Jake followed with a right hook to the guy's cheekbone. A crunch greeted his ears.

Claire stopped the water flow, but Jake didn't slow his attack. He grabbed the tweaker's shirt and pulled him in close.

The maniac had killed Kendall and terrorized Claire. He'd destroyed the sense of safety and comfort she'd fought so hard to create. Jake planned to enjoy making him pay.

Blood leaked from the man's nose, droplets dotted his green shirt. Jake leaned in until they were nearly nose to bloody nose. "Nobody messes with Claire. Got that?"

"It's mine. She was supposed to give it to me. It's mine! That stupid bitch Kendall promised to give it to me, but she reneged. She couldn't be trusted, just like her mother."

The man spit blood into Jake's face. He brought his arms up and broke the hold. They faced off and circled each other.

"I think a broken promise is the least of your worries right now." Jake wiped the glob of spit and blood off his face with the back of his hand. This wasn't his first fight against someone who didn't play by the rules. Fine with him. Jake tried to keep himself between the killer and Claire behind the bar. He wouldn't leave her vulnerable. One way or another, he'd take this psycho out. He brought up his arms in a wrestling take-down position and charged.

Oh. My. God.

Claire tossed the hose into the sink. Her stomach twisted as the two men slugged it out. When would Hank get here? She'd pressed the panic alarm on the hostess stand five minutes ago. Dread made her body heavy. What if the Voice of Doom had cut the alarm?

The men crashed to the floor with a bang. The killer came out on top and pummeled Jake. Her heart stopped. It revved up again when Jake pushed the Voice of Doom off and assumed the dominant position. She couldn't wait any longer.

She grabbed the first weapon she found—a heavy glass beer pitcher from the drying rack. The only problem? What in the hell was she supposed to do with it? If only she...

The gun.

Grunts and groans filled her ears. She dropped to her knees to find where the gun had fallen. Frantic, she felt along the floorboards. She cheered silently when she saw it near the bottom of the ice machine.

Exalted, she swiped it off the floor. She stood, spread her feet shoulder width apart and bent her knees slightly. The gun felt cold when she gripped the handle with both hands. Her first impulse was to shoot, but she couldn't risk hitting Jake. She raised the gun toward the ceiling. Her heart hammered as she waited for the Voice of Doom to separate from Jake.

She hurried around to the front of the bar. The fighters seemed evenly matched. Jake was a bit bigger, but the maniac had enough meth-fueled crazy in him to negate the weight advantage. They grappled on the floor, turned into a small round table, knocked it down. The killer rolled on top of Jake, but he flipped the other man off his body and the men separated. Both breathing hard, they sized each other up like boxers at the beginning of the tenth round.

Doubt seized her. The gun trembled in her hands. What if she missed? What if she hit Jake instead? Her heart pounded in her ears. There may not be another chance. She had to do it now.

Claire lowered the gun and aimed at the Voice of Doom. Willing her hands to calm, she eased the trigger back. The gun cracked to life and bounced her arms back.

The killer shrieked. A warm serenity soaked through her body as blood spread across the seat of his jeans. She'd hit him in the ass.

It was just a flesh wound so the danger he posed wasn't past. They couldn't afford for him to realize she wasn't as cool and collected as she pretended.

"You bitch! You shot me!"

Bile rose in her throat. She'd gone hunting with her father as a girl, but she'd never hit anything. Now she'd shot a human being. Sure, he was a tweaked-out psychopath, but still she'd pulled the trigger and put a bullet in a person. The reality of it all made her nauseous. Counting to twenty, she pushed back her inner turmoil into a closet in her mind. She slammed the mental door shut. She'd deal with it later.

"You." She continued to aim the gun at her human target. "Hands on your head." Isn't that what they always said on TV?

He shot her a scathing look, rolled to his stomach and intertwined his fingers behind his head. "This is not right. Why is everyone so against me?"

"I don't think anyone is particularly thrilled with you right now." She pressed back against the bar for support, worried her shaky legs wouldn't hold out much longer.

Jake stood guard over him. "We need to tie him up. Anything handy nearby?"

"Suzie's got a bar apron back here. Why don't you use that to tie his hands behind him?"

"Yes, ma'am." Jake kissed her on the top of her head and walked behind the bar to search for the apron.

Her stomach calmed somewhat, but her arms began to ache unbearably. Who knew guns could get so heavy, so fast?

"Got it." Jake came back around, trussed up the man's feet and wrists and reached for his cellphone. He leaned down and whispered something in the killer's ear.

She couldn't hear the words, but they must have had their desired effect. Jake stood and laughed, a cold sound masquerading as humor. The man's body stiffened.

Claire lowered the gun to the bar and sank onto a stool. Her stomach twisted and cramped. She laid her head down on the dark wood. The cool surface calmed her riotous nerves, gave her a chance to think for a moment. She'd made the right move. Really, she never had another choice.

Sirens cried in the distance. With a relieved sigh, she slid off the stool. Her knees shook a bit, but she maintained her somewhat wobbly stance. She'd always heard it seemed like forever for law enforcement to respond. Now she understood what that meant.

"You okay? You're not looking so hot." Jake tilted his head.

Now was not the time to flake out. She'd have plenty of time for that when she finally made it home.

She tried to look reassuring, but her calmness wavered. "It's over."

"Ha!" the killer croaked from the floor. "You have no idea what you're in for now, Honey Child. By this time tomorrow, you'll be laying—"

Jake ended the tirade with a kick to the psycho's stomach. Though bloody and battered, the killer looked...happy. His face lit by some evil inner light, he looked like someone who taunts you because he knows the best secret in the world but has no intention of sharing it.

"Honey, just look at your choice of lovers to know all is not right with your world. They always leave you in the end. Always."

His maniacal laugh made her take an involuntary step back. Her throat constricted.

"I should have killed you last night at the house. I'd have saved you a lot of heartbreak. Literally."

Jake squatted down and slammed his fist into the Voice of Doom's face, silencing the killer.

Chapter Eleven

"Looks like you only grazed him," the EMT muttered as she packed up her equipment and stuffed it into a navy and black duffel bag.

"Maybe I'll have better luck next time." The words were out of Claire's mouth before she had a chance to censor them.

The EMT looked up as she unwound a stethoscope from around her neck. Her severe French braid pulled her face tight, but couldn't help with the bags puffing up underneath her exhaustion-dulled hazel eyes. They were the serious eyes of a woman who'd spent too many sleepless nights trying to keep the dying alive.

For a moment, Claire could hear her own heart beating as it pounded in her chest. Damn. Why couldn't she think before she spoke? She opened her mouth to say something, anything, to mitigate the callousness of what she'd just said but nothing came out. Instead, she stood there with her mouth agape like a fish flopping around on the bottom of a boat.

The EMT looked away and stuffed the stethoscope into a zippered pocket. "Yep. I heard about this one. You probably don't remember, but I was here the night you found that girl. We brought her to the morgue." She closed the bag and slung it over a shoulder. "I wouldn't blame you if you shot him right between the eyes. Just next time, even though officially I hope there isn't a next time, please shoot him in the next county. I don't like having to patch up tweaked-out murderers." She gave a terse nod and joined her partner at Harvest's door.

Claire stared after them as they walked out into the parking lot. She envied them. They got to escape the Voice of Doom. She had to stay in the same room with him until the investigators got a chance to talk to her. Unease crept along her skin as he watched her from across the room. Because of his injury, he remained on the floor surrounded by deputies. Their presence did little to ease the fear scattering her thoughts as her muscles tensed.

The blood that had seeped through the right back pocket of the Voice of Doom's jeans jarred Claire's mind back to Saturday night. Dried blood matting Kendall's hair. Fear grabbed ahold of her heart and she squeezed her eyes shut. Stark terror rose up, took her back to that night.

"Do you understand these rights as I've read them?" The deputy's voice sounded too loud to her ears.

"I'm not an idiot, of course I understand, Officer Donut."

His snide tone triggered the memory of the first threatening phone call. Tears pushed against her closed eyelids. A familiar helplessness descended over her. Just like that night, she was scared and unable to protect the people she loved.

She shivered and Jake tightened his arms around her. The heat emanating from his body soaked into her cool skin. She'd almost gotten him killed pretending he was her bodyguard with benefits. How could she have done that? How could she have been so selfish? Gritting her teeth, Claire choked back a sob.

For forty-eight hours she'd lived on the precipice of disaster. Through it all, she'd held on to her anger with an iron grasp and let it guide her actions. She'd refused to show how scared she'd really been.

The click of the handcuffs locking around the killer's wrists exploded her tough-girl facade.

Claire lost it. Fat tears cascaded down her cheeks and her shoulders shook from her efforts to stifle her sobs.

Jake turned her around in his arms and pressed her cheek to his chest. His hands stroked her hair.

"Let it go, Claire." His lips brushed the top of her head. "Just let it go."

It poured out of her. All the fear and frustration ran down her face in hot tears that dripped off her chin. Jake rubbed her back in circular motions. His touch anchored her to him. Somehow she understood that he'd hold her until the tempest insider her ran its course.

For a few minutes the world consisted of Jake and her, the deputies working around them forgotten. She basked in the comfort he provided and snuggled in deeper. His responding sigh set off a fluttering in her stomach.

Everything she needed in life was wrapped around her.

The realization came to her crystal clear and fully formed, as if someone had spoken it aloud. Suddenly, the warmth in her body vanished. Her breathing turned heavy as she sucked air in and out, unable to fill her lungs. Her arms tingled. Fighting off a wave of dizziness, she pushed away from his chest.

She promised herself after Brett that she'd never need someone else that much again. The idea of needing Jake scared her almost as much as the events of the past two days.

"What's wrong?" Worry lines creased his forehead.

Her line of sight narrowed. Focused on his slate-blue eyes, her peripheral vision turned dark. Her fight-or-flight response surfaced, demanding release. Unable to form words, she jerked away from him and stumbled backward until she smacked up against a barstool.

"Claire, we need to take you down to the station. The investigators can talk to you there so you don't need to wait around while he's here." Hank dipped his head toward the Voice of Doom, whose gaze bored holes into her.

She inhaled several deep, cleansing breaths. Her heart slowed and her surroundings came back into focus. She grabbed Hank's hand tight in her own.

"Jake, Sgt. Carlyle will take you over in a bit." Hank ushered her toward the door.

"Claire." Jake's voice rang out above the deputies' chatter and the snapping of the forensics guy's camera flashes.

She glanced back, unprepared for the determined set to his square jaw. Before she could process what it meant, his face softened. His signature smirk set off fireworks inside her. She fought against the instant buzz of attraction but, her nipples tightened.

"We'll talk later." There was no question in his words.

His challenging tone set off a warm flush that heated her chest.

"Promise me, Claire."

Even if he wasn't here for the long haul, he wanted him. Needed him. For her, it wasn't just physical. She yearned for the total package. Her heart skipped a beat. "I promise."

ာ•ာ•ာ

A relieved sigh escaped as Claire sank back down onto the cheap vinyl couch in Hank's office. She could sleep tonight without every light in the house on. The sound of her phone ringing wouldn't set off alarm bells. A giddy excitement buzzed through her body, she couldn't wait for everything to be normal again.

Absentmindedly, she picked at a one-inch tear in the stiff fabric. A seed of discontent bloomed. It wasn't really over. Not yet. She had to know why it had all happened. She wasn't leaving the sheriff's office until she did.

Beth had told her once that juries didn't like to convict unless there was a motive. Apprehension squeezed her upper back tight. She rolled her neck and stretched her shoulders, but the muscles remained coiled. If he went free, he'd make good on his promise to hurt her and her family. Dread wormed its way into the recesses of her mind.

She would spend the rest of her life looking over her shoulder, waiting for the moment when the Voice of Doom would appear. She shuttered. If he didn't spill his guts to the investigators, she'd have to find the phone and flash drive. If juries wanted motives, she'd find one. There was no way this psycho would stroll out of jail ever again.

An antsy she could shake itched its way up her spine and she paced around Hank's office as she chewed her bottom lip. She'd been hanging out in the cramped space for the past hour, ever since the investigators finished talking with her. They'd introduced themselves as Strunk and White, no first names, asked her a few questions and released her right as the first-shift deputies were heading home for dinner.

The walls of Hank's office closed in on her as she marched around the small space. She had to get out of here. Waiting and worrying was making her nuts.

She grabbed Hank's coffee cup and hustled out the door. The fluorescent bulbs, sizzling above the hallway's Army-green vinyl floor, intensified her hungry headache. Her stomach growled for dinner, a snack, anything. Maybe she could snag a donut in the break room.

Anything would do, but the apprehensive little girl inside her cried for comfort food: creamy mashed potatoes, lasagna stuffed with meatballs, warm chicken noodle soup, anything made with chocolate. Unfortunately, she'd have to placate her hunger with the vending machine's heart-attack-in-a-plastic-sack food.

Hank's oversized "I Heart Nebraska Football" cup quivered in her hand as she strode down the hall. Already, she'd had four cups of strong coffee. Caffeine ran through her veins faster than a rabid dog chasing a squirrel. Still, she jonesed for more. The joys of addiction.

She half hoped and half dreaded running into Jake in the hall. She hadn't seen him since the deputies separated them at Harvest for questioning.

"My name is Frank Darcy and I want to call my attorney."

That voice. Every hair on her body stood at attention. Frank Darcy? Burlington had told the truth about Kendall's biological father.

Appetite forgotten, she jerked to a stop. Where was he? If she could listen in on the interview, she wouldn't have to wait on Hank for the answers. A quick glance around confirmed no one else would see her eavesdropping. If she got caught, there would be hell to pay, but it would be worth it.

To her left, a door stood ajar. She tiptoed over and stood with her back flat against the wall. Craning her neck, she caught a glimpse inside the video room. Hank and two deputies crowded around a black-and-white TV watching the closed-circuit feed from the interrogation room.

"Look, Barney Fife, I said I want to call my lawyer. Give me a phone. Now."

Small speakers attached to the TV added static to Darcy's cynical tone. Hearing him talk and watching him on the grainy footage sent a cold blast of fury across Claire's skin.

The murdering jerk slouched back in his chair and dismissed the investigators with a turn of his head. Strunk and White sat across a narrow table from him. An unopened case file filled the space between the two sides.

He looked as if he didn't have a care in the world. The EMTs must have shot him full of some pretty damn good meds to even out his meth high. If he worried about going to prison for murder, it didn't show on his face.

The cup handle cracked in her tight grip. She'd shoot the bastard in the ass again if she had the chance. Of course, at the time, she'd been aiming a bit higher. Nervous about hitting Jake, she'd flinched.

Too bad.

"Sure, sure. You'll get your call," Strunk said. He smiled. No malice touched his face.

Judging by his companionable attitude, she figured he played good cop.

"Course, we'll have to put you into lockup until he gets here. It'll only take, what, five hours for him to get here from Denver. Sound right, Steve?"

White cracked his knuckles. "Yep."

"It's a pretty drive, what with everything turned nice and green from last night's rain. The lawyer might stop for dinner. Maybe even at Harvest. The wife has been begging me to make reservations there for months. Your attorney, he might check into a hotel. Be here what, around nine tonight?"

"Yep." White lumbered over, stood behind Darcy. A feather couldn't have fit between his protruding belly and Darcy's shaved head.

"You'll have to spend the night. Deal with the drunks pulled over after Monday Night Football. Might get puked on. Man, those are nice shoes you've got. Hate to see what regurgitated nachos and beer would do to them." Strunk paused, flipped through some papers. "So why don't you talk with us a bit first. Dragging in a lawyer only slows the process down."

Darcy and Strunk faced off against each other in silence. After a few moments, Darcy leaned forward, his face a mask of gullibility drenched in sweat.

"Really? You think my lawyer-free cooperation would make your DA look kindly on little ol' me?"

Sarcasm thick as honey, but nowhere near as sweet, coated Darcy's words.

"Now, Frank...can I call you Frank?" Strunk leaned forward, hands open, palms showing.

"You can call me Sugartits McGee if it makes you happy. But I'm not talking without a lawyer. Phone. Now." He crossed his arms in front of his chest.

Good cop looked straight into the camera, shrugged his shoulders. Without a word, he gathered his papers and left the interview room.

Frustrated, Claire wanted to holler at the men in the video room. They couldn't just give up. They had to make him talk.

White strolled to the door, paused and looked back at Darcy. "Hope that bandaged butt of yours starts feeling better soon, Sugartits."

Out in the hall, Claire fought to stifle her chuckle. She lost. It bubbled out of her before she could cover her mouth.

A hand flung the video room door the rest of the way open. Hank glowered at her from inside the doorway.

Oh, crap.

She'd survived the psycho in the next room, but now her own brother looked as if he were going to kill her. She held out his coffee mug like a peace offering.

"Coffee?" Her cheeks ached from her smile's fake sugary goodness.

"You need to go home. Now."

Hank's hand pushed against the small of her back as he forced her down the hall.

"Hank, just let me talk to him. He'll talk to me, I know it."

The vein in his neck went into overdrive, pulsating like a jackhammer. He'd clamped his jaw down so hard, she worried he'd break a tooth.

"No." The single word from Hank came out low and slow.

She scrambled for another option to find out why Darcy had killed his own daughter. Was there really access to three million dollars out there somewhere on a flash drive? "How about the interview video? Can I watch it? I could point out and similarities between how he talks now and during the phone calls he made to me."

Hank opened the door to his glass-encased office and grabbed his empty mug from her hand before walking inside and barring her from following him. "No."

"What if—"

"For the last time, no! You are not sitting in on the interview. And no, you can't watch the video of it. Now go home." Hank slammed the door in her face.

She wanted more information. She needed her pound of flesh. Riled up and ready to continue the argument, she grabbed the doorknob.

"Get away from my door or I'll arrest you for being a pain in the ass." Hank's muffled words made her jump sky high.

She spotted him glaring at her through his office window. The stern look on his face and the stubborn set to his jaw showed he meant business. She stomped her foot in frustration.

"That's not a real charge, Hank. Let me in."

He yanked the blinds closed.

Exasperated, Claire kicked at the blue plastic recycle bin next to Hank's door. She missed. Her sandal flew off her foot and sailed down the hallway.

Perfect. Just perfect.

She clomped over to her shoe, the slick floor cool against her one bare foot.

"You know that could be considered attempted destruction of government property." A touch of deadpan humor lightened Jake's words.

She froze with her sandal in one hand, bare foot angled up toward her knee. Warmth flowed through her, wrapped around her shoulders and melted her irritation. Her skin tingled and her fingers ached to touch him.

Bodyguard with benefits. What had she been thinking? There was no way she could ever touch this man again and keep her heart. Hell, she could barely be in the same room with him without wanting to throw herself into his arms.

She'd only known him for a few days. He lived hundreds of miles away. They were both too headstrong to function together as a couple. In her experience with men, the thrill wore off quickly. They got bored. They cheated. She couldn't go through that again. To protect herself, she had to walk away.

Half heartbroken already, Claire turned. Her resolve wavered at the sight of him. His hair spiked up in all directions as if he'd spent the last hour running his fingers through it. He'd missed a button on his shirt when he'd hastily gotten dressed earlier. Had it only been a few hours ago that they'd been on their way to buy condoms? Heat blasted up her body at the memory.

That damn smirk tugged at the right side of his mouth. "He locked me out too." He stood at the end of the hallway, two steaming cups in his hands. "Coffee?"

Her stomach lurched. She'd downed too much already. Any more of that cheap, bitter brew and she'd spew. Not the lasting impression she wanted to leave him with as he walked out of her life. "I'm good. Thanks."

An awkward silence fell. Neither moved.

Baffled by the whole situation, she had no idea what to say or do or feel. She'd never gone from sex to shooting before. Hell, she'd never come on her desk before with someone she'd only known a few days and wouldn't know for much longer. She needed to escape.

"Well then, I guess you're heading back to Denver soon. Have a safe drive." A cold brick settled on her heart. She had to get out of here before she started crying again. Hanging her head she trudged down the hallway toward the door. One problem. She had to get by him.

"No." His firm voice halted her feet.

Her head popped up as her pulse increased. "No?"

He put the coffee down on an empty shelf. A frisson of sexual heat sparked between them. His body called out to her like a siren, luring her toward a dangerous and rocky coast. Afraid her heart would be broken on the shore, she kept her eyes lowered.

"You promised we'd talk later." He trailed a finger down her cheek. "I thought you were the kind of woman who kept her word."

Blinking back unwanted tears, she forced her wobbling lip to still before gazing up at him. It scared her how badly she wanted to spend even a little more time with him. A vague picture formed of what a future with Jake would be like. Coming home to him after closing Harvest for the night. Crawling into bed and snuggling up against his warm body. Ruthlessly, she tried to push away those thoughts but they lingered.

She should walk away now and make a clean break of it, but she couldn't do it. Missing this time with Jake would haunt her. She'd recovered from a broken heart before, she could do it again. Probably.

Heat enveloped her fingers as she intertwined them with Jake's. Her hand looked so small and fragile in his, like delicate china laid atop an oak table. They shouldn't go together, but they did. "Let's go."

Jake delivered a soft kiss to the top of her head and dumped the paper coffee cups in a nearby trashcan. Together, they strolled out the door, hand-in-hand, into the gathering dusk.

Chapter Twelve

*H*ow is it that you own a restaurant and don't cook?" Jake took a pan down from the overhead storage rack in Harvest's kitchen. They'd ended up at the restaurant after a short detour to the Stop and Sip because of Claire's barren refrigerator at home. After the day they'd had, he figured they could both use some comfort food.

"I ignore the recipe and add in a little of this and a little of that." Claire shrugged. "When I'm in the kitchen I just can't follow directions." She handed him half a dozen eggs.

He snorted. "Yeah, no shock there."

"Very funny."

Out of the corner of his eye, he watched her survey the ingredients on the metal prep table. Eggs. Bread. Cinnamon. Vanilla. Who didn't like breakfast?

"You're making French toast? And you mock *me* for not knowing how to cook?"

He raised an eyebrow. The girl talked enough smack to play in the NBA, but the give and take excited him, made him curious to find out what she'd say or do next. Until he'd met Claire, he didn't realize how boring his dating life had been. The old man had been harping on him for years to look beyond the willowy blondes Jake had always dated, to find someone who had pluck and passion. His little fairy warrior didn't have a passive bone in her delectable body.

He slipped his hand around her slender waist and pulled her to him until her back nestled against his chest. She snuggled in as he tucked her head under his chin. "Don't knock the French toast 'til you've tried it." She relaxed against him, molded herself to him. A perfect fit.

As if he'd been zapped with Viagra, he hardened instantly. He toyed with the thin, red spaghetti straps of her dress resting on her shoulders. He slid a finger under one, tracing its path across her warm, supple skin. He wanted to sweep the food off the prep table and eat her instead. As if reading his thoughts, her stomach growled its disapproval.

Damn.

He chuckled into her coconut-scented hair. The aroma launched a fantasy about lying on the beach next to her. Her string bikini would barely cover her heavy tits. A little paper umbrella would float in her Mai Tai. She'd wrap her luscious lips around the straw and suck while he rubbed sunscreen all over her decadent curves. It would be paradise.

Her stomach growled again, louder this time.

Reluctant to let go of the fantasy, he waited a beat before lifting his head. "Did you bring Onion with you?"

"Oh, shut up." A flush rose above her neckline like a blinking neon sign declaring: Look here.

He squeezed her shoulders and laid a quick kiss on the top of her head, inhaling the tropics again. "Come on, go get me a bowl to whisk the eggs and I'll satisfy your stomach. The rest, I'll take care of later."

"Yes, sir." Claire winked at him. "Didn't your mother teach you to treat the kitchen help with more care?"

A familiar ache squeezed his heart. He stared at the stainless steel prep table, not wanting her to see what ate at him. "No. She left when I was two. Haven't talked to her since."

Her small hand wrapped around his. "Jake, I'm sorry."

Looking down into her face, he knew she was. No pretense lay hidden in her wide eyes or in the concerned twist of her mouth. If she said it, she meant it. He could get used to that. Part of him already had.

Uncomfortable with the realization, he turned away. "Yeah. They divorced. I grew up with my dad. It worked out great." He knew this speech by rote. "Two guys in a guy house."

She put the bowl down in front of him and handed him an egg. Her hand lingered, so soft and strong at the same time.

"I found her." His voice cracked. He'd never told anyone before, not even his dad, but he wanted—no, needed to tell Claire. "I was seventeen and about to graduate high school. It seemed like something I had to do. I'd been working at Absolute with dad since I was old enough to file, so it really wasn't very hard to do a records search."

He remembered the excitement mixed with foreboding as his fingers had flown across the keyboard. He must have looked over his shoulder a million times to make sure his father couldn't see the screen. It had only taken a few minutes and boom, he'd found her.

"She'd gotten remarried a few years after she left us. They lived on a ranch two hours outside of Denver. I told my dad I was going to a concert with friends and drove out there. I parked my truck on the side of the road, down a bit from their dirt driveway. There was a mailbox there. I figured she'd have to get the mail eventually. She did. She looked a bit grayer, heavier than dad's pictures, but it was her."

His gut had wrenched when she'd checked her mail. He'd looked down at his white knuckles wrapped around the steering wheel as hate and love spun around inside him in a confused whirlwind. Even now, the picture of her reaching into that battered metal mailbox put a hitch in his breath.

"Then I saw the school bus in my rearview mirror. She waved as it slowed down. A boy and a girl got out. Elementary-school age, both of them. And she smiled at them, hugged them. She loved them. I could see it."

The profound sense of rejection had hit him like a slap across the face. Ever since, with every emotionless hookup and cold, calculating move, he'd distanced himself from the women who floated through his life.

Until now. Until Claire.

Jake looked down. He'd crushed the egg Claire had given him, the slimy yolk dripping from his fingers. "I must have left marks on the road, I took off so fast."

She handed him a towel. "Did you ever go back? Contact her at all?"

He shook his head and tossed the dirty towel onto the prep table. "No. That part of my life's over. Doesn't matter anymore."

Thankfully, she said nothing to that. He locked up his teenage-boy hurt and cracked the rest of the eggs into the bowl in silence.

He had breakfast-for-dinner whipped up in no time. Claire sat on the prep table eating with gusto. He forgot all about his food when a syrup-drenched piece of French toast left a trail of sticky sweetness on the corner of her mouth. Her tongue darted out to swipe at it. Unable to get it all that way, she wiped up the rest with her middle finger and sucked it off.

His body went on high alert. His pulse hammered and blood rushed through his veins, engorging his cock. He thought he had been rock hard before, now he worried his zipper wouldn't hold.

She caught him staring with his fork frozen halfway to his mouth. Turning beet red, she dropped her gaze. Then a devilish smile tugged at the corner of her mouth.

Trouble. Just the kind he liked. He waited, food forgotten, anxious to see what she'd do next.

She parted her cherry lips and her gaze darted over to him. She blew him a kiss and then...she hummed.

What the hell?

Dumbstruck, he watched her eat the last bite of French toast.

She hopped down from the table, strutted over to the industrial sink and dumped her plate. She grabbed a tiny square package from a shelf and tossed it to him. Without looking his way, she slipped off her red dress and left it puddled on the floor. Claire sashayed down the hallway, her swaying ass framing the jade-green thong.

Jake could live to be a hundred and he didn't think he'd ever see a sexier sight. Her voluptuous curves nearly overwhelmed his senses. He couldn't wait to trace a finger across her peach nipples and slide into her wet folds. His balls tightened when her butt jiggled as she strutted away.

Then she looked back over her shoulder, a come-hither look in her chocolate-colored eyes.

"Coming?"

Was he ever.

He looked down in his hand. A condom. She must have snuck it into their grocery bag at the Stop and Sip when he hadn't been looking.

He jerked his head back up. For a few beats, Jake watched her saunter down the hallway. Unable to resist the view any longer, he rushed to catch her.

She unhooked her bra and dropped the flimsy scrap of silky material to the hallway floor. Lust slammed into his stomach and then sank lower, making his cock harder than the cast iron pan he'd used to make the French toast. The brief side view of her heavy, round breasts as she turned into another room sent all his blood straight to his dick. His body reacted like that of an untried fifteen-year-old boy. It had been a long time since a peek of side boob had pre-cum staining his boxers.

Damn. Claire astounded him, body and mind. Even with the light-purple bruise on her cheek, half hidden behind her waves of red hair, she was the most beautiful woman he'd ever seen. He didn't know when or how, but he'd make sure Darcy paid for punching her after setting her Jeep on fire. But right now, Darcy was in police custody and a naked Claire waited for him somewhere down the hall.

He found her in the employee lounge. A leather couch lined one wall. Humming refrigerator, sink and counter lined the other. In the middle stood Claire, her inviting nipples pointing toward him. She crooked one red painted fingernail at him.

Jake crossed the room in two long strides and wrapped her up in his arms. Her puckered nipples poked his chest through his shirt and sent fire through his veins. He leaned down, capturing her sweet mouth with his. He teased her mouth open, the syrup lingering on her tongue promised of sweeter things to come. Nectar from the gods couldn't have tasted better.

He ran his hands down her back, cupped her soft ass and pulled her against his groin. Pleasure so intense it almost hurt exploded in him as she ground her damp pussy against his jeans. He almost came from that friction alone.

She moaned into his mouth. Her fingers dug into his taut shoulders as she stretched herself upward, arching into him.

The need to bury himself inside her, hear her call out his name again, almost overwhelmed him. He lifted his head.

The heady look in her eyes shot him back to the moment when he'd held her at the railroad tracks after she'd first confronted Darcy. Her red hair had been flying every which way, her face starting to bruise and dirt streaking her cheeks. She'd been through hell, but remained undaunted. He'd been so turned on by her fiery spirit, he'd wanted to secret her to a dark corner and fuck her senseless. She had felt the same, judging by her diamond-hard nipples and her do-me look. He'd managed to stop himself, just barely, telling her they'd regret their actions. He'd been an idiot.

"I was wrong," he mumbled as he kissed the spot below her earlobe. "I'm not going to regret this at all."

She laughed, low and breathless as her ample breasts rubbed against his chest. Her fast fingers unbuttoned his shirt setting off shocks. The pleasure nearly overwhelmed him and he let out a groan of his own.

Lifting her against him, he reveled in how good she felt in his arms. Determined to make her his, he carried her to the couch. Sitting back on the smooth leather, he kept his hands on her fleshy hips as she straddled him. Her breasts swayed, tempting him. He licked one erect nipple and closed his lips around the hard nub. She moaned and arched her back, digging her fingers into his shoulders.

Letting go almost killed him, but he had to get out of his clothes. She slid to his side on the couch. They continued to kiss as he yanked off his shirt, buttons flying everywhere, and stood.

Their hands battled at his waistband. She won. He shucked off his shoes as she unbuttoned and unzipped his jeans. With anxious fingers, she slid his cotton boxers and jeans to his ankles. Entranced by the gleam in her eyes, Jake kicked them off.

Looking down, he saw the tip of her pink tongue lick her luscious lips, his cock pointed at her. She took him into her warm, wet mouth. His vision went black. His knees nearly buckled. Her talented tongue lapped at the pre-cum glistening against the head of his cock and had him ready to explode. He stepped back and brought her pliant body up.

She sucked on her bottom lip, pushed him down to the couch. Her fingers toyed with the strap of her thong. The red of her fingernails against the green of her underwear reminded him of Christmas. She was one package he couldn't wait to unwrap.

He looked up at her body silhouetted in the harsh fluorescent light. For anyone else, the lighting and angle would have been unflattering, but not his Claire. He was bewitched by the confidence and strength hidden beneath her sexy-as-hell body. An invisible force kicked him in the gut.

"What are you doing to me?" he whispered.

She slipped her thong over her creamy hips and let them fall down her long legs. "Making you happy."

"Good, I was afraid you were trying to kill me."

She smiled. "They do call it the little death."

Claire took the condom from his hand. She ripped the package open and slid the latex on, her fingers unrolling it down the length of his cock. The light touch of her fingers teased his erection and made it throb.

Looking at her hand curled around the base of his dick, he worried he'd come from her fingers alone. He tried to convert fractions, remember the preamble to the Constitution and anything else he could think of to stop himself from shooting right then.

When she straddled him and lowered herself onto his rigid cock, he could have died a happy man. Her warmth tightened around him and desire tightened his balls. Pleasure rippled outward from where they joined. He dragged a thumb across her peach nipple and pinched the nub lightly. Entranced by the sight of her delicious breasts, he held a rounded peak to his mouth and sucked on the large nipple.

Small whimpers escaped her lips. She increased the pace, riding him hard and fast. Her moist pussy ground against him as she enveloped him in smooth, deep strokes.

"More," she cried.

Happy to oblige, he flipped her onto her back and thrust deep into her hot, silken pussy. His body awash in sensation so pleasurable it had him trembling, he tried to slow down to make it last, but her fingernails dug into his back in protest. Her hips met his every thrust, wild passionate cries escaping her lips. Like this, locked in each other's arms, they fit. Perfect.

"Claire." Her name came out in a strangled cry as he neared the abyss. He couldn't hold on much longer.

Her inner muscles undulated against him and squeezed. Her whole body tensed in his arms as she came around his dick, screaming his name to the ceiling. His balls tightened and he buried himself to the hilt. He came inside her with the force of a tidal wave, moaning his release into her hair.

In that moment of blissed-out clarity it hit him— he never wanted to leave.

ৎ৽ৎ৽ৎ৽

Claire brushed her fingers through Jake's soft black hair. His head lay nestled on her shoulder. He'd flung an arm across her waist; the weight of it warmed her, like the world's sexiest security blanket. She relaxed until her bones were the consistency of melted butter. All was right with the world.

Content and satisfied, she willed herself not to think. She reined in any imaginings of before or after, of what could or couldn't be. There was only right now.

"I don't want to move ever again." His breath tickled her neck.

Claire empathized completely. "Eventually, you'll have to."

He rose up onto his forearms. "Why? Am I squashing you? I don't want to hurt you."

True, her stomach and ribs still ached a bit from the Voice of Doom's kick by the train tracks and her wrist remained stiff, but that wasn't the hurt she worried about. She didn't see any way Jake could avoid making her heart ache. It stung already. She sucked at the whole not-thinking thing.

"What is it?" Concern shone in his eyes.

Talking about him leaving would only make it seem more real. She wasn't ready to push open the curtains of reality. "I need to go freshen up."

"Hurry back." He nipped her earlobe. Kissed it better.

In the doorway she paused and looked back. Jake lay on his back. An arm rested across his forehead. He was so tall, he barely fit on the couch. Tears sprung to her eyes. She blinked them back. Tomorrow would be soon enough for that.

She scooped up her bra from the hallway and grabbed her dress off the kitchen floor. Slipping it on, she trudged to the dining room bathroom, her heavy heart making every step an effort.

The toilet wouldn't stop running as she washed her hands. She walked into the stall and jiggled the handle. The water continued to rush inside the porcelain tank.

Great. Like I don't have enough falling apart in my life right now.

Claire lifted the heavy tank lid to adjust the flush valve.

She gasped. Her heart stopped beating for a moment.

A plastic sandwich bag lay at the bottom of the tank. It had sunk so far down, it forced the valve to stay open. A phone and flash drive were visible inside the clear plastic Baggie.

Holy crap. I've found it.

Chapter Thirteen

*C*laire twirled around and performed her happy dance in the claustrophobic bathroom stall. It was part hip shimmy, part ass shake and all celebration. She'd found it. Giggling, she added some shoulder bounces to the soundtrack playing in her head. Sure, she'd discovered it by fluke, but still she'd found it!

"Jake, come in here! You won't believe what I found!"

The phone and flash drive were wedged in the valve so that water continuously rushed into the tank but didn't accumulate. Even though the tank held only an inch of water, plucking the plastic Baggie from its depths skeeved her out. Grimacing, she dipped her hand into the tank, grabbed it with the tips of her fingers and pulled it above the water line. The information hidden away on the phone and flash drive had caused so much misery. Her heart skipped a beat.

Bad vibes hovered in the air. Goose bumps dotted her bare arms and she flicked her gaze around the bathroom, looking for the source of her discomfort. She half expected to find Darcy tucked away in the corner, ready to pounce. But he was in police custody. No one lurked in the shadows ready to kill her for the information on the devices. Still, anxiety buzzed in the back of her mind like a tiny mosquito.

She stared at the plastic sandwich bag, unable to rip it open. A person died because of this phone and flash drive, the information they held could still pose a danger. Her logical side urged her to stop being so namby-pamby and open the damn thing.

Legally, she needed to get the phone and flash drive to Hank. She knew that. But there was no way she'd give it to him before finding out what information was worth Kendall's life. Too much had happened to ignore the answers in her lap. She shrugged; she'd find a way to explain it to Hank.

She unsnapped the bag and yanked out the pink phone. Without pausing, she pushed the button to power it up. Kendall's smiling face stared up at her. The dead girl's arms hung around a frat boy's neck, her eyelids at half-mast. They wore New Year's Eve hats. An extended party blower jutted from Kendall's mouth. It pointed at Claire like an accusing finger.

"Jake, where are you?"

A pan clanked against the kitchen floor.

"You okay? Do you need help?"

Another small crash sounded. "I've got it."

Judging by his gruff tone, Claire figured her offer must have offended his testosterone-required pride. Men.

Intent on her discovery, she shook the canary-yellow flash drive onto her palm. What if it really did hold the key to three million dollars? The thought blew her away. She needed to get to her laptop. Clutching the evidence, she hightailed it out of the bathroom.

She glanced down at the cellphone photo, certain she'd done right by the girl. "Don't you worry, Kendall. We got him."

Her attention glued to her prize, Claire turned the corner into the kitchen and tripped. Her knees pounded against the floor. Pain erupted in her kneecaps as violently as an egg exploding in the microwave.

"Shit!"

Dragging in a ragged breath, she looked over her shoulder to see what she'd stumbled over.

Jake lay unnaturally still in the threshold.

The earth stopped spinning as anguish squeezed out the rest of the world. Had he tripped and fallen against the dish rack? That would explain the earlier noise.

Ignoring her aching knees, she crawled over to him. "Jake!"

His eyes remained shut. He didn't move, not even to flinch at her panicked cry.

The right side of his face appeared red and swollen. A deep gash above his right eye dripped blood onto the floor. She dabbed at the blood, relieved to see him jerk back when she touched his injury.

"Thank God, with all that's happened you scared me there. Jake, are you okay? Talk to me." Desperate to elicit a response, she grabbed his shoulders and shook him.

He groaned and blinked, smiling slow and easy. The fear tightening her chest eased a bit. She caressed his cheek and he lifted himself to his elbows. Her heart traveled back from her throat to her chest. She remembered to breathe again.

"What happened?" His words slipped out in a woozy tone. Confusion danced across his face for a moment. Desperation soon replaced it. He grabbed her wrist in a tight squeeze.

"Claire, get out. Get out now." His words were a hard whisper.

"Wha—"

A throat cleared behind her and an intense and immediate dark haze of terror thickened around her. She jumped up and spun around.

"You're not going anywhere." The voice, low and rusty, sent a chill careening up her spine.

She took stock of her enemy. The man was huge, like professional-wrestler big. His shiny bald head sat on top of a nearly nonexistent neck. A diamond stud, at least a carat in size, sparkled in his ear. He clenched an extinguished cigar between his teeth, its foul stink wafting out from his black T-shirt.

But it wasn't his image that freaked her out the most. No. It was his gaze, unemotional and cold, that told her everything she needed to know.

He'd come here to kill her.

Panic ripped through her body at the realization. Claire bolted for a weapon. She had to protect herself and Jake.

The thug yanked her up by the straps on her dress. He held her so high her feet barely touched the ground. She lashed out. Desperate to escape, she kicked her legs backward. Aiming for his nuts, she only connected with his concrete thighs.

"Hel—"

His hand clamped over her mouth, cutting off her scream.

She squirmed as he pulled her in, holding her tight against his chest. She tried to elbow him in the ribs, but couldn't get the leverage. His right arm held her to him in an iron grip, trapping the hand holding the phone and flash drive to her chest.

Terrified, she struggled in his arms but couldn't get away. Sweat made her arms slick as she twisted and squirmed. She shrieked into the palm covering her mouth. Hysteria filled her. Escape. She had to get out. Her gaze darted around the room, seeking salvation.

Like an answered prayer, Jake pushed himself up and made it to his knees, but the goon leveled a solid kick to his side. He crumpled to the floor.

An adrenaline-fueled frenzy took over Claire's body. She yanked her arms against the giant's vise-tight grip. Like a trapped animal, her sole focus became freedom.

"Stop moving or I'll make it hurt more," the giant rasped.

His threat intensified her need to break free. She kicked her legs, connecting with his knee. He didn't even flinch. Out of the corner of her eye, she saw Jake labor to get up. His slow movements gave her hope, provided the impetus to fight on. She flailed against him, but her captor ignored her ineffective jabs and kicks. Instead his gaze locked on Jake.

"Stay down." The thug kicked him in the head, knocking him to a prone position. "I'll be back for you."

Jake lay unmoving, his jaw slack. She went rigid with fear. His chest's erratic jerks up and down were the only signs of life.

Transformed into a wild woman, she clawed at her captor's muscled arms. She slammed the back of her head against his sternum. He barely grunted.

The goon flipped Claire over his shoulder like a fifty-pound bag of dog food. Grasping the phone and flash drive in one hand, she beat her other fist against his back. She tugged up his black T-shirt and scraped her fingernails across his exposed flesh.

"Keep doing that, bitch, and I'll kill you for fun."

He lumbered out of the kitchen toward Harvest's dining room.

She grabbed the doorframe and clung to the beveled wood, but his forward motion continued. Her fingernails scraped across the wood. Splinters embedded under her nails, making her scream out in pain.

But she refused to give up. He'd kill her no matter what she did. Well, he'd have a hell of a fight on his hands.

She screamed for help. The dining room's noise-reducing ceiling tiles absorbed her cries. Fighting against the panic threatening to render her immobile, she knew she had to escape.

Flailing, she knocked over table tents describing the week's specials. Her hand dragged across a smooth tabletop. Desperate for any weapon, she grasped a set of silverware. Letting out a guttural yell, she lifted it above her head and with every ounce of power she had, she plunged the knife and fork into the goon's lower back. They sank into his flesh like a knife gutting a suckling pig. Blood spurted from the wound.

"You bitch," he roared.

He threw her down. Pain rocketed through her head as it bounced against the wood floor. Stunned, she couldn't move. But it only took a moment for abject terror to motivate her muscles. Her head foggy, she lurched onto her feet and scurried back.

Reaching around with a meaty hand, he plucked the bloody utensils from his back and flung the knife and fork down. They clanked against the pine floor.

"You'll pay for that." He thundered after her.

Claire turned and ran as if the devil himself were at her heels. She weaved around tables, aiming for the panic alarm on the hostess stand. His footsteps pounded closer.

If she could just push the button, she and Jake would be safe. Hank would be there in a matter of minutes.

She stretched her arm forward, but went sailing backward.

Gripping her hair in his hand, he tossed her to the floor. He stood over her, his chest heaving and his face flushed. Veins bulged from what little neck he had. Quick as lightning, he leaned down and backhanded her across the face.

For one heartbeat she felt nothing except the certainty that this was going to hurt like hell. In the next moment, throbbing agony took over. Her teeth felt as if they'd been knocked loose.

"You'd better pray I don't need stitches, bitch."

Her survival instinct in control, Claire kicked him in the balls. She had enough time to get up to her feet and turn toward the kitchen. But not enough to take a step. He cuffed her again in the head. She staggered.

Looking into the goon's eyes, she saw only death. He snarled at her. A strange sense of calm came over her, as if she had become an observer instead a participant in the melee. Everything around her came into greater focus. The colors became brighter and her thoughts registered faster.

There were only two things this thug wanted more than her head on a silver platter, the phone and the flash drive. But without them, investigators wouldn't have a motive for Kendall's murder. Darcy could walk away a free man.

"You ready to die?" He growled the words.

No. She wanted to live. For once, she wouldn't just react. Too much was at stake. She'd play it smart, save Jake and avenge Kendall.

In a last ditch effort to survive, she threw the phone and flash drive in one direction then ran in the other. She didn't stick around to see what he decided to go after. She had to get to the kitchen. Once there, she'd get Jake. They could escape out the delivery entrance.

Her bare feet slapped on the tile floor. A second set echoed her own.

Shit.

Claire dashed toward the kitchen. But he was faster. His hand locked around her wrist. He whirled her around. The malevolent gleam in his eye made her breath catch. She tried to pry his fingers off of her, the whole time hearing someone scream in the distance.

The goon popped her in the face, sending her sprawling to the floor. "I said shut up your screaming."

It hadn't been someone else yelling. That panicked crying had been from her.

He hauled her to her feet and dragged her toward the door. She fumbled along, her vision blurry. Blood dripped from her nose down her chin. He paused by the hostess stand, squatted down and swiped the phone and flash drive off the floor. The small devices disappeared into his fleshy hand.

She couldn't go out into the parking lot. Hank had always told her the biggest mistake some victims make is to get into the killer's car. She had to fight to her last breath.

"You'll never get away with this."

"I already have."

He pulled her out into Harvest's dim parking lot, lit only by streetlights. A sedan idled near the Dumpster. A sense of déjà vu echoed through her. Another night, another violent predator, and once again she was prey.

He didn't look at her. His focus was on the sedan. She could tell from his body language that he had dismissed her as a frail, broken girl who wouldn't fight back anymore.

Damn, it pissed her off. She may be small, but she sure as hell wasn't weak. He thought she was; most people did. But maybe this time, she could use that to her advantage. They were only a few steps from the car. It was now or never. She held her breath and let her whole body turn to jelly.

The action jerked the goon off balance, brought his face closer to hers. She slammed the heel of her palm against his nose. Blood squirted everywhere.

Flush with success, she pulled away from him, fighting for freedom. But his meaty paw clung to her wrist.

Jake's eyes snapped open. At first he had no idea why he was on Harvest's kitchen floor. Then the memories rushed in.

He had pulled on his jeans when Claire had called his name from the bathroom. Her squeal of delight had captured his attention and he had shuffled down the hallway, pulling his shirt on as he moved. He'd only made it a few steps into the kitchen when the guy slammed into him from behind. The rest still registered as a blur.

An image that came through with clarity though was Claire's concerned face looking down into his. His heart had lifted at the sight of her. But his spirits had sunk faster than the *Titanic* when he had spotted his assailant looming behind her tiny frame. And he hadn't been able to help her.

His body tensed and his pulse went into overdrive. He tried to push himself to a sitting position but dizziness enveloped him and he collapsed onto his back. She needed him. He wouldn't fail her. Not again. Furious at himself, he jerked into a sitting position. A wave of nausea washed over him. He held his breath until it passed.

He hated himself right now. The guy had beaten the crap out of him and taken Claire. He'd failed her. Disgusted, he realized, he had no idea how long ago that had happened. But he had to find her. He'd promised her she'd be safe with him. Some protector he'd been.

His peripheral vision was for shit. What he could see had a slight halo around it. He shook his head as he pushed himself upright.

Claire's scream for help echoed through the restaurant, followed by a man's roar. Jake's gut constricted. She was still here. He wobbled forward on rubbery legs. He had to get to her. Save her.

Aching, he staggered farther into the kitchen looking for a weapon. A bonanza of choices awaited him.

Jake grabbed a cast-iron skillet and dashed into the dining room, fury feeding his need for vengeance. But he was too late. They weren't in the dining room. He sped past a set of bloody cutlery. Blood rushing in his ears, he dashed around overturned chairs. From the looks of it, Claire had put up a hell of a fight.

He spotted them in the parking lot.

The assailant tugged Claire toward a black sedan parked near the Dumpster. Jake sped out the door clutching the skillet like a baseball bat. His bare feet had just touched the asphalt parking lot when he saw Claire's body go limp. His steps faltered.

But half a second later, she slammed her hand into the man's face. Blood gushed from the attacker's nose. A proud smile spread across Jake's face.

That's my girl.

Too bad the asshole wasn't hurt enough to let her go. Jake mentally shrugged. Claire's blow had been enough to distract the intruder from hearing Jake's approach. That was all the opening he needed. Neither noticed him as he came up behind.

The man pulled Claire's battered face close to his. "Time to pay."

"My thoughts exactly." Jake smashed a cast-iron skillet against the man's skull.

It made a dull thunk upon impact. The assailant fell to the ground in a heap, silent and unmoving. Jake dropped the skillet and reached for Claire. The pan clanked as it bounced off the asphalt. The goon didn't flinch. He was out cold.

Pulling her to him, he buried his nose in her auburn hair. Despite everything, the scent of coconut soothed away his anger and worry. Unwilling to take even half a step away from her, he clutched her to his body.

Their lips met in a flurry of unspoken emotions. He wanted it all to come through, all the things he couldn't find the words to say. The fear that had twisted his insides when he thought he'd been too late. The bone-melting relief when he folded her in his arms. The lust that had somewhere along the way transformed into love. The truth of that reality electrified him.

She broke the kiss. Laid her cheek against his chest. Unsure of what he should say, how he could tell her, his mind went blank. He blurted out the first thing that came to mind.

"Sorry I wasn't here sooner."

She tilted her face up. "Yeah, your timing could have been better." She grinned at him.

He wiped her bloodied nose clean with his thumb. Pain flashed in her eyes.

"Claire, I'm so sorry. I should have—"

"Shh." She dusted his bruised face with a flutter of small kisses. "We're quite the pair."

He grinned down at her. He'd talk to her later, find a way to get her to move to Denver. Now that he'd found her, he wasn't leaving Dry Creek without her. He glanced down at the unconscious man at their feet.

"We've gotta call the cops."

Claire grabbed the phone and flash drive from where the goon had dropped them. A deep crack split the cellphone's screen and the buttons didn't respond to her fingers. "It's not working."

"Come on, our phones are inside."

She wavered a bit. He clasped her hand in his and they hurried to the restaurant. Energy coursed through his body as he planned how to talk Claire into leaving her hometown.

As they mounted the steps, a figure emerged from the shadows. "It seems your services are no longer required, Mr. Warrick."

A sense of inevitability settled in Jake's stomach. This case had so many twist and turns, this last one just seemed par for the course. Claire looked up at him. Shock and confusion etched on her pretty but bruised face.

"Claire, let me introduce you to Kendall's father. This man pointing a Smith and Wesson at us is Charles Burlington."

જીજીજીજી

The synapses in Claire's brain shuttered to a stop. She gaped at Charles Burlington. Why did Kendall's father have a gun?

He wore a dark blue suit. Even in the dim light, she could tell the expensive fabric had been tailored to his lean frame. A red tie twisted into a Windsor knot sat snug against his throat. His crisp white shirt showed nary a wrinkle.

His conservative outfit stood in sharp contrast to the matte-black handgun he pointed at them. She couldn't wrap her mind around it.

"Ms. Layton, I presume?" His tone had an Ivy League snobbish quality to it that spoke of boarding school and ski homes in Vail.

Her gaze traveled up to his face. Strands of gray streaked through his dark brown hair and hinted at his age, but his forehead remained suspiciously unlined. His lips compressed to form a hard line. Her heart stopped when she looked into his eyes. A determined finality shone out from them.

Her mouth went dry. She fought to make her tongue function. "Y...yes."

"When Kendall informed her mother that she was giving that drug addict three million dollars of my money, we both knew it was only a matter of time. But Kendall was her father's daughter. I assumed it would end badly for her."

The world zoomed in and out of focus. She wanted to puke.

"You assumed your own daughter would get killed and did nothing to stop it?" Barely restrained outrage trembled in Jake's voice.

"I most certainly did not." Burlington's face darkened. "She was adopted."

Revulsion spread through Claire's body like a heat wave. The cold-blooded bastard.

She wanted to tear him apart limb from limb but Jake tugged her closer to his strong bulk.

"Gun." His hushed tone brought her attention back to the problem at hand.

Unable to claw out Burlington's eyes, she seethed, "You're a real piece of shit, Burlington."

"Women should not use such vulgar language. It is unbecoming of your gender."

"Want me to shut her up?"

Claire started at the goon's low rumble. For a big man who'd been knocked out cold a few minutes before, he moved with unnerving quiet. He looked as if he'd been shot out of a cannon and was completely pissed off about it. Without thinking, she eliminated any space between her and Jake.

"No, Mr. Franklin, we'll deal with Mr. Warrick and Ms. Layton inside." Burlington tilted his head toward Harvest's door. "Shall we?"

She turned to Jake, his features as hard as granite. A vein bulging at his temple was the only give away to his state of mind.

"Why don't you lead the way, Franklin?" Jake smirked and stepped back to let the big man go first.

The giant grunted at Jake's request.

"No, Mr. Warrick. You and Ms. Layton go right ahead. Please sit down at a table in the dining room."

Fear shook within her. The odds were not in their favor. They were outgunned and vulnerable. She wanted to make a mad dash for it, go with her gut and pull a kamikaze attack. The impulse nearly overwhelmed her, but it would be suicide.

She had to think, formulate a plan. If she rushed Burlington or the goon, Jake would back her up, but she doubted they could win in this situation. She couldn't risk getting him killed. He meant too much to her for that.

With the giant at their backs and a gun aimed at their heads, their only option was to follow orders. Stiff with rage, she strode into the restaurant with Jake by her side.

She glanced up at him as they crossed the threshold and his mask slipped. For the briefest moment she saw the anger eating away at him, then his iron facade fell back into place. She squeezed his hand.

They'd come out alive after facing down a gun before. They'd do it again.

Chapter Fourteen

*D*o not be an imbecile, Mr. Franklin. Put the gas can away and go get the bag of candles out of the sedan." Burlington quirked his eyebrows at Jake. "Finding good help is a never-ending endeavor. You really were a promising employee, Mr. Warrick. I dislike having to let you go."

"Yeah, I can tell your heart's breaking." Jake squeezed his hands into tight fists. Fury burned just underneath his skin and demanded release, preferably by pounding Burlington's face to a bloody pulp.

Burlington leveled the Smith and Wesson at Jake. "Tsk, tsk, Mr. Warrick, sarcasm is the sign of an uneducated mind. I thought you were better than that."

"Now *my* heart's breaking." Jake stretched his fingers wide and sought out Claire's hand.

Her fingers held tight to his larger hand. Leaning his head over until her soft, red hair brushed against the side of his forehead, he inhaled her coconut shampoo. "You antagonize while I figure a way out," he whispered.

She squeezed his palm twice in quick succession.

"You know you won't get away with this. I'll hunt you down until you pay for what you let happen to Kendall." Claire's voice heaved with indignation.

Burlington let out a frustrated huff. "My dear Ms. Layton, Kendall was not some poor waif tossed asunder by the cruel world."

Jake scanned the dining room for a weapon. The need to protect Claire overwhelmed all of the worries about what could happen to him. He had to figure a way to get her out of here. The hostess stand with its hidden panic alarm stood a good four feet away near the door, with Burlington standing between him and both options. He'd never be able to smash a chair onto Burlington's head before the man got off a round.

"No." Burlington turned the gun so it centered on Claire. "My adoptive daughter brought the end upon herself."

"Really? I never knew someone could bludgeon themselves to death and toss their own dead body into a Dumpster," Claire scoffed.

Training his gaze forward, Jake covertly swept the table top behind his back with his fingertips, hoping to nab a set of silverware. A steak knife wasn't his weapon of choice against a Smith and Wesson, but he'd take what he could get right about now. Moving at the speed of a snail to keep his actions a secret from Burlington, he inched his fingers across the polished table. All he touched was wood. Angry at himself at being caught unaware and unprepared for the umpteenth time in the same day, he returned his empty hand to his side.

"You, Ms. Layton, are an unpleasant woman."

"Have you taken a look in the mirror lately? You're not so awesome yourself."

While Claire snarled at Burlington, Jake kept his gaze locked on the gun. Burlington had it pointed in their general direction, but seemed to have forgotten about it. Jake could cut the space between them in three strides.

"Yeah, I don't think the father of the year committee has knocked on your door lately, if ever." Claire lobbed the insult at Burlington like a grenade.

His face reddened as she continued to mouth off. No doubt about it, she let loose plenty of venom when angry. He knew what it was like to be on the receiving end of one of her diatribes. It almost made Jake feel sorry for the son of a bitch. Almost.

"That is quite enough, Ms. Layton. I believe you have some things that belong to me. Please put the phone and flash drive on the table."

"No." Claire's chin rose and she slid her hand clutching the devices behind her back.

"Do not be foolish. Hand over the items and I shall promise not to personally harm you or Mr. Warrick." He held out his hand toward Claire, empty palm facing upward. "Chop, chop."

Jake snorted his disbelief. Burlington couldn't even arrange his face into a pretense of innocence. The attempt at humble innocence made him look deranged.

The goon, Franklin, rumbled back into the restaurant. Plastic grocery bags crinkled in each of his large hands. He paused in the doorway and light from the parking lot outlined his roided-out body. Time had run out. Jake tamped down the adrenaline spiking his blood. He had to remain calm and in control if they were going to make it out alive.

Franklin lifted a bag. "So, where you want 'em?"

"The table is fine for right now. You have the needles?"

His stomach tightened. Needles were not a good sign. Jake saw the color drain out of Claire's face. He smiled down at her and hoped she didn't notice the worry eating a hole into his gut.

A burst of cinnamon apple infiltrated the room. Jake guessed it originated from the bags Franklin had dropped onto a nearby table.

Burlington's gun hand twitched. The slight movement provided a tell-tale sign that someone wasn't as comfortable with a handgun as he wanted them to believe. The idea made Jake curl his lip in a smirk; finding a chink in someone's armor always made him happy.

"Your silence does not bode well for your answer, Mr. Franklin." Burlington tapped his foot impatiently. "Where are the needles?"

"In the car." The big man kept his eyes on the floor.

Burlington pursed his lips and rolled his eyes to the ceiling. His jaw went rigid.

Jake's spirits rose. Finally, something was going their way. If Burlington blew up at his bodyguard, Jake had to be ready to take advantage of the situation. He dropped Claire's hand and moved a half step in front of her. His arms hung loose at his sides.

Burlington turned his gaze toward Jake and the hairs on his neck spiked. One false move and this would go south real quick. He had to get Claire out of here.

"Mr. Franklin, this type of negligence will not be tolerated. If you cannot improve yourself, you will not be accompanying Mrs. Burlington and me to South America. Get the needles now!" Red spots of frustration dotted his cheeks.

"Yes, sir."

Without another word, the thug shuffled out into the parking lot.

Burlington swiveled the gun back to Claire. "My patience has grown thin, Ms. Layton. Put the phone and the flash drive on the table."

Claire hurled the devices at their tormentor. They flew by Burlington's head, missing him by at least a foot, and bounced off a round dining table.

Quick as a snake, Burlington fired a bullet into the hardwood floor. The wood cracked beside her feet.

Claire screamed as she jumped into the air.

Fear grabbed Jake's heart and squeezed. Her scream vibrated inside his head. Panicked, he shoved her shaking body behind him, primed to launch himself at Burlington.

"You look quite savage, Mr. Warrick. I suggest you not act out the violent fantasy playing in your head." He cocked the gun. "As for you, Ms. Layton, if you knew the women in my life, you would know that I am quite practiced at dodging missiles." He shrugged his shoulders as if the entire situation was all too common for him. "Take a seat, both of you."

Clair huffed behind him and flopped down into a chair. "Bastard."

Jake eased into the seat next to her, on the lookout for an opportunity to at least get her out of here. He didn't mind taking his chances, but he wouldn't risk her life for a bit of evidence.

Franklin trotted back in, his face flushed. The goon must not be used to running in the summer heat. Either that or his head still ached from the omelet pan Jake had cracked against the big man's skull.

The giant clasped a small envelope-sized black case in one gargantuan fist. "The needles."

"Put the needles on the table, Mr. Franklin, then go stand next to Ms. Layton. We don't want Mr. Warrick to forget what is at stake here."

Claire flinched when Franklin moved beside her, cigar smoke and sweat floating like an invisible cloud around him. The asshole chuckled.

Shame and anger boiled in Jake's veins. Some fucking protector he'd turned out to be. How could he let her down like this? They were stuck between a breathing rock and Burlington's Smith and Wesson.

Burlington reached into his pocket with his free hand and drew out two zip-ties.

"Shit," Clair said under her breath.

"There is no need to whisper, Ms. Layton. I am rather impressed with these pragmatic items." His lips twisted in wry amusement. "I admire its unassuming efficiency. Too often my colleagues get wrapped up in convoluted schemes to defraud their clients, showy actions that land them in jail. Simplicity is the key to a successful scheme. Whether it is little old ladies, pension managers or small-town police officers, give them a plausible and easily understood explanation for cash losses and they will accept it."

Fuck. Sweat slid down Jake's spine as dread solidified in his belly. Burlington had no plans to leave them tied up while he split.

"Ah, I see understanding dawning in your eyes, Mr. Warrick. When you quit, the answer to why was obvious. You had the flash drive and were planning to use the information to access the three million dollars yourself. No one walks away with my money. No one."

"That's not true, not everyone is as big of a crook as you are. Anyway, the flash drive is incidental, worthless to anyone but you." If Jake could keep Burlington talking, he could increase their chances for survival.

"That is where you are woefully ignorant. The Cayman Islands bank account codes on the flash drive will give anyone access to my funds." Burlington shrugged his shoulders.

"The money you stole from the little old ladies and pension funds?" Claire's soft words hung heavy in the air.

He marveled at the innocent curiosity in her voice. She might not know his plan's details, but she played along as if she never doubted it would work.

"Of course not." Burlington's voice rose an octave. His jaw tightened and he took a menacing step forward. Then, as if recalling himself, he released a quick breath and smoothed his expression into a mask of superiority. "Stealing is a repugnant activity. I paid myself a bonus percentage of the market profits they wouldn't have gotten without me."

"That's a one-way ticket to prison." Jake would enjoy seeing this weasel in an orange jumpsuit.

"Only if the police find out about it, which is why Kendall had to be silenced." He jerked his head in a firm nod.

"She was blackmailing you." The pieces came together in Jake's head. The money manager had been adamant the phone not fall into anyone's hands but his.

"Yes." Burlington shook his head. "It is extremely distasteful to discover the child you reared and sent to the finest boarding schools would stoop to something as low-class as extortion." Burlington sighed and shrugged his shoulders. "She had extraordinary technical skills and hacked into my accounts. She downloaded everything she needed to try to bleed me dry."

"That's why you let Darcy kill her?" Jake asked.

The zip-ties rested in Burlington's hand. The gun pointed to the floor. Burlington was caught up in telling his tale.

"Termination was not a part of the original plan, but there is little in this world that Mr. Darcy cannot mess up. We had hoped Kendall would give him the flash drive and phone as she had promised him. Then, Mr. Franklin would take care of him and return the items to me. Neither of us realized just how far Mr. Darcy's methamphetamine paranoia had progressed."

If Jake took a run at Burlington, Franklin would try to save his boss, leaving Claire free to escape. As far as plans went, it wasn't a great one. But he didn't have time to come up with anything better. They needed to act now.

He straightened up in his seat, adrenaline pumped through his body. He doubted he'd make it out alive, but he'd go down saving her. A fair trade.

He forced his breathing to slow. Kept his sights on Burlington. Tracked Franklin out of the corner of his eye. His body was primed and ready to take action.

"It was a simple plan. The only difficulty was keeping the truth from my wife, who I doubt would be pleased, even if it *was* necessary. Charlotte is more than my wife; she is my partner, my soul mate. Why, just thinking of her makes me anxious to move forward with this endeavor so we can be together again on the beaches of Brazil, enjoying our millions." He took a step forward. "Mr. Franklin, if you will be so kind as to restrain Ms. Layton. I do believe Mr. Warrick will be more cooperative if his lady love is...how shall I put it...effectively detained."

Claire gasped and dropped Jake's hand, drawing his attention away from Burlington. In the dim light, he couldn't make out her features exactly, but he didn't need to. The image of her storming into Harvest's bar a few days ago, her temper running at full steam, was enough.

He hadn't come to Dry Creek looking for the woman of his dreams, but he'd found her anyway. A redheaded firecracker with a smart mouth, a fast brain and a body that had him praying for X-ray vision. If he died saving her, she needed to understand the sacrifice was worth it to him. Grasping her face in his hands, he lowered his lips to hers.

A powerful hand pulled against his shoulder, fingers digging into his flesh, but Jake refused to be torn away from Claire.

"No, Mr. Franklin, let us allow them this moment. Our social mores demand that every condemned person be granted one last request. This is theirs."

Burlington's words danced on the edge of Jake's consciousness. His focus centered on Claire. He put everything he wanted to say into that kiss. From the moment he'd tapped her on the nose, he knew he'd never be the same. He'd been bewitched by her fiery hair and luscious curves. She'd captivated him with her stubbornness and passion. Her sarcastic, quick wit had mesmerized him. She was his warrior pixie.

"I love you, Claire Layton."

Her dazed look sharpened. It morphed from understanding to horror.

In one fluid movement, he stood and jammed a finger into Franklin's eye socket.

The big man howled in pain and slapped his hand over the injured orb. Jake whipped around, pulling Claire up. "Run."

She hesitated. Fearing she'd die by his side, he swung her by the arm and catapulted her past Burlington.

Burlington's head snapped around, following Claire.

Ready to inflict serious damage, Jake barreled toward Burlington.

Chapter Fifteen

*C*laire inhaled heaven.

Granny Marie's apple strudel must have just come hot out of the oven. Its cinnamon scent permeated her bedroom. Exhaling, her stomach rumbled and her mouth watered in anticipation. In a few minutes it will have cooled enough to eat. This time she wouldn't rush in to cut off a slice and burn her mouth on a steaming apple. For once, she could wait. Anyway, her toasty-warm bed was too comfortable to leave.

Rolling onto her back, she reached for the covers to snuggle deeper. Her heavy arms slid across her warm body. There were no covers, only her bare skin sticking to slick leather upholstery. The truth unfolded slowly. She wasn't in bed. No. It must be the couch.

Had she fallen asleep in the living room and kicked off the blanket in the night? How had she ended up sleeping on the couch? Had she been watching a movie? Struggling to remember, her thoughts moved as if they were mired in honey.

A crackling, popping noise snapped in the distance. Why would Granny Marie be making popcorn for breakfast? It didn't make sense, but Claire couldn't grasp why. Everything seemed off, but she couldn't put her finger on it.

As she stretched, a tingling sensation burned up both arms. Damn, she must have slept on her stomach with her arms trapped underneath her. She flexed her fingers, trying to increase circulation in her numb limbs.

Only half awake, Claire sniffed the air hoping for another burst of cinnamon apple. An unexpected richness snuck in with it. She wrinkled her nose. Olive oil. Why did she smell olive oil? Straining to open her eyes, confusion swamped her sleep-addled head.

A sudden tension coiled tight in her stomach. She needed to do something, but what? A glimmer of the truth lay just beyond her mind's reach, but like a half-remembered dream, it floated in her subconscious, swaddled in a fog.

Again, she tried to pry her eyes open, but the lids were too heavy. Panic ratcheted up her heartbeat, her blood rushed in her ears. Something was wrong. Why couldn't she open her eyes? Why was it so hard to move? She tried to call out for help. Her tongue, thick and heavy in her mouth, hampered her efforts and only a soft moan came out.

Struggling not to lapse back into a dazed state, she inhaled deeply.

Smoke invaded her lungs. Choked her. Coughs racked her body as her lungs gasped to inhale clean air.

The violent spasms jarred Claire fully awake. Her eyes snapped open. She couldn't make sense of what she saw.

She was on the couch in Harvest's break room.

Naked.

Jake lay nude at her feet.

Candles, so many candles, surrounded them, their wicks alive with fire. It looked like a romantic tryst gone desperately wrong, as if they'd passed out after making love.

An oily trail dotted the hardwood floor, leading to the room's only exit. Smoke snuck in under the door in a skinny column of gray.

Everything came back to her. Jake had poked Franklin in the eye, thrust her toward the door and gone after Burlington. As he had struggled with Burlington, the goon recovered enough to rush Jake. All three had gone down. Unable to leave him like that, she'd run full throttle into the melee. They'd rolled in a ball of flailing arms and kicking feet, chairs and tables knocked over by the combatants.

In the middle of the brawl, a sharp object had pricked her leg. Ice had surged through her veins and her body had gone slack. Though her vision had turned hazy, she'd seen Burlington looming above her, a half-filled needle in his hand. She'd wanted to lash out at him, but couldn't lift her arms or legs. Helpless, she had sunk into a sea of desperation.

Unable to move, she had stared up at the ceiling while the skirmish had gone on around her. Fighting the effects of the drug, she had turned her head in time to see Burlington plunge the needle into Jake's shoulder. He'd reared back and roared before collapsing to the floor.

She'd wanted to reach out to Jake. Touch him. Brush his hand with hers. But the drug was too powerful. Her vision turned dark. Unable to move or see, only her hearing connected her to the world.

"The other vial broke when the table flipped over. Half a dose will have to do for them both, Mr. Franklin. Take them to the break room and strip them. Light the candles in there. You will start the fire with whatever is flammable on the premises. It is a restaurant; it should not be hard to find something that will do the job." Burlington had paused, his footsteps pounding on the hardwood floor away from her and toward the backdoor. "This cannot look like arson at first blush, Mr. Franklin. Do not disappoint me in this. Oh, and one final thing..."

At that point, she had fallen completely into the void. Saw nothing. Heard nothing. Felt nothing. Until now.

Terror ripped through her. She had to wake up Jake. They had to get out. She sprang up. Too quickly. The room wavered before her. Afraid if she closed her eyes, she wouldn't get them open again, Claire concentrated on the doorknob. Silver. Round. It seemed so far away. She counted to twenty and tried to keep her breathing steady as smoke filtered in under the door.

The room stopped spinning. She slid off the couch to the floor beside Jake. Curled up on his side, he slept-off the drug. His hands were clasped and tucked underneath his chin. He'd already suffered a probable concussion from his multiple run-ins with Franklin. What the hell had been drugged done to make it worse?

What if she couldn't wake him? She doubted her sluggish muscles could pull him out of harm's way. She could barely move her arms enough to stroke his face.

"Jake! Jake! Wake up. We have to get out of here." Smoke burned her esophagus and another coughing fit shook her body. "Jake! Wake up. Now!"

The tingling in her limbs lessened. Grabbing his bare shoulders, she leaned in close to his face. Her mind raced as panic swamped it, but her sluggish body moved in slow motion. Cursing her inability to wake him, she laid her forehead against his and prayed for a miracle.

Her nose rested against his as she gathered her strength to try again to wake him. In any other situation she wouldn't have been able to stop from sneaking a kiss. "Jake! Wake up now or we're both going to die!"

His eyeballs rolled under his closed lids. She held tight to the hope his reaction offered. Her muscles pulled and ached, but they were under her control again. Digging her fingernails into his tender skin, she shook him by the shoulders. "Come on, Jake! Wake up! We have to get out of here!"

"Five more minutes, baby," he mumbled.

"Jake Warrick, you get up right this moment or so help me God I will leave your naked ass in the break room to burn to death."

His eyes popped open at her meaningless threat. The terror riding roughshod through her body released its grip. She smiled despite the dire circumstances.

"Why would I burn to death?" A second later he sniffed the air and realization dawned in his gaze. He shot to his feet, and immediately fell to the couch.

"Give yourself a minute. I don't know what Burlington shot us up with, but it does a number on you." Claire grabbed her sundress and pulled it over her head. "Where are your keys?"

"Jeans." His face glowed with a distinct pale-green tinge.

189

She found Jake's clothes in a pile beside the couch. She dug his keys out of his pocket and tossed the jeans to him. He put them on with deliberate care. Dazed, he stayed focused on the task, but his skin had gone back to its normal tan. Her thong was balled up on the floor by Jake's shirt. She leaned against the break room table and lifted a leg to put it on.

A squeal of twisting metal followed by a loud crash stopped her in the middle of slipping on her underwear. Jake jumped up from the couch. He stood firm on his shoeless feet.

"The metal shelves by the prep table." She sank down against the table. Her restaurant. Her fucking restaurant was going down in flames all because of some asshole's greed. Everything she'd worked for, all the hours she'd spent, all the money she'd scrimped and saved, it all burned on the other side of that door. She'd never hated anyone as much as she loathed Burlington right now.

"How do we get out?"

Claire swung her head around. Jake stood, fully dressed, only inches from her. She gulped down her pain and finished pulling up her thong under her dress. "Turn left out the door and we can get out the delivery entrance. It opens up to the alley. If they're still in the parking lot, they won't be able to see us."

Jake lowered his head and crushed his mouth to hers. His strong lips delivered the kind of searing kiss meant to embolden her spirit, not entice her body. Brief and intense, like a shot of passionate courage, it did the job. By the time he broke the kiss, she'd regained her emotional footing.

Bucked up, she set her sights on the door. "Let's do this."

The doorknob warmed her palm but didn't burn it. Cautious, she turned it and opened the door an inch. Jake peered through the slight opening.

He pushed it shut. "There's smoke, but I couldn't see any flames. Are there any towels in here?"

Claire pulled two orange dishtowels from a drawer near the sink. She wet them and handed one to Jake. They tied them around their heads bank-robber style so only their eyes showed. He reopened the door, sank down to his hands and knees and crawled into the hallway. She dropped to all fours and followed close behind.

A pitch-black darkness enveloped the windowless hallway. The bastards must have cut the power and knocked out the back-up generator. That meant no sprinkler system, no emergency lights, no fire alarm and no one coming anytime soon to hose down Harvest.

Dry Creek's population deserted Main Street most Mondays after five p.m. It had been near nine p.m. when she'd found the phone and flash drive in the bathroom. She couldn't begin to guess how long had passed since Burlington sent her to dreamland.

If she had any luck, and in her heart she knew she did not, dawn had arrived and Margret Goodwin was about to open her bakery shop across the street. That busybody would call the fire department and everyone else in town. Maybe the firefighters would arrive before Harvest burned to the ground. Damn. She'd never hoped to be the subject of Margret's telephone gossip tree before.

Smoke irritated her eyes, but she fought to keep them open. She could make out the barest glimpse of Jake's outline ahead of her. A coughing fit took hold of her, shook her entire body down to her toes. In her attempt to gulp in oxygen, she sucked the towel into her mouth. Whipping it off, she dragged in a ragged breath. Tainted air burned its way down her esophagus and spread through her lungs like wildfire tears across the plains.

The combination of smoke from above, fire behind and darkness surrounding them became overwhelming. Trapped in an inferno, panic gripped her and her lungs tightened. Another hacking spasm rocked her body. The walls closed in around her. Overwhelmed with confusion, she second-guessed everything.

Did they turn right or left out of the door?

What if they had turned the wrong way?

The hallway wasn't that long. Shouldn't they be at the door by now?

Frozen by indecision, she stilled. The approaching fire heated her back, but didn't burn. Not yet.

"Claire, where are you?" Jake's disembodied voice traveled through the dark.

She couldn't see him, but her heart held onto his voice like a lifeline. It tugged her forward. Right hand. Right knee. Left hand. Left knee. She repeated the process away from the flames and toward freedom.

The drugs and smoke inhalation had zapped her energy. She collapsed by the heavy metal door. Jake sat, his back leaning against it. Seeking his strength, she pulled herself to his side and laid her head on his shoulder.

"It's locked. Is there another way?" His drug-slowed voice tickled against her ear.

"Keypad." The single word scratched her raw throat. The keypad deadbolt lock used its own battery not connected to Harvest's power source or the generator. With luck, Burlington had missed it.

She pushed her listless body up, balancing against the door until she stood straight. Blindly, she patted the wall, searching for the keypad to unlock the door. She ran her fingers across the invisible pad, imagining the location of each button, and punched in Harvest's ten-digit phone number. A vibration buzzed her hand as a small door slid open, revealing the deadbolt knob. Holding her breath, she turned it. A quiet click chimed.

The smoke was so thick she could barely get any words out as she sank to her knees. "Try the door."

Jake stood and weaved a bit before pushing against the door. It opened soundlessly. Fresh air washed over them both like a cleansing rain. Claire sucked it deep into her lungs, desperate for survival. Coughing, she edged into the alley.

"Wait here, I'm going to go check out the parking lot." Jake scurried off, looking much better than she felt.

She glanced back down the darkened hallway. Flames danced at the far end of the hallway, eating their way up the walls. All her bravery drained out of her weary body. It took every ounce of her strength not to give in to the despair, sink to the ground and weep.

She'd worked so hard to maintain the historical aspects of Harvest, including hardwood floors and hand-carved wooden detail work along the ceiling. It had taken months to talk the reticent local farmers who provided most of Harvest's food into posing for the photos lining the stairwell. Her mother had helped pick out the autumn color scheme that permeated the restaurant, from the burnt-orange towels to the deep-purple nametags. The bar—that gorgeous, Western-style bar. She'd been like a kid at Christmas when the workmen installed it. All of it was now just fuel for the fire.

Tears soaking her smoke-irritated eyes, Claire watched the blaze march toward her. Even though heat poured out of the open doorway, she shivered with chill. Her mind shut down as her heart shattered into a thousand tiny pieces.

"They're gone," Jake panted as he raced to her side. "Come on, Burlington said something about South America. I'll bet you my hockey season tickets the asshole is getting ready to pilot his jet south. The regional airport is fifteen minutes from here. Come on, we might still catch them."

He backpedaled toward the parking lot, but Claire couldn't move. An unexplainable protective instinct pushed her to stay with Harvest as it went down. She couldn't leave it alone as flames shot through the roof any more than a parent could leave an injured child. Harvest was her baby.

She jumped when Jake's hand brushed away the tears she didn't realize had been flowing across her cheeks.

"I'm so sorry, baby. I know you want to stay, but the bastard who did this may still be at the airport. We can call the fire department on the way."

A whoosh exploded in the kitchen and the flames burst forward like a fiery fist. Jake yanked her backward, away from the flames racing down the hallway toward them.

Anger squeezed her tear ducts shut. There was nothing she could do to save her restaurant. Her dream had turned to ash.

The need for vengeance grew inside her soot-filled chest. Like the fire before her, the rage started as a spark but built quickly, destroying every other emotion in its path. Burlington would be held accountable. He'd pay for it all. Nothing and no one would stand in her way.

Claire set her shoulders and clamped her jaw tight. Heat licked at her face as she stepped back into the gravel strewn alley and walked away.

Chapter Sixteen

*T*he blaze shrank in Jake's rear-view mirror as he sped down the deserted Main Street away from one disaster and, no doubt, straight into another.

The digital clock on the dashboard read twenty minutes after midnight. The town had rolled up its sidewalks, the first bit of good luck they'd had in days. With no traffic in sight, he kicked the accelerator to the floor, speeding through four red lights and ignoring the doubt creeping into his thoughts about their chances of success. Everything came down to this moment. They had to get to the regional airport before Burlington escaped.

Tucked safely in the passenger seat, Claire tossed his SUV's manual to the floorboard as she groped inside the glove compartment for the cellphone. He'd gotten two at the store the day before on a buy-one-get-one-free deal.

"Got it." She slammed the compartment shut and sat back in her seat. Jiggling her leg, she chewed on her bottom lip and kept her gaze locked on the sleek, silver flip phone powering up.

He reached out, clamped his hand down on her bouncing knee. "We'll make him pay for all he's done. I promise."

Her bare knee stilled beneath his palm as he massaged her smooth skin. Although he stayed focused on the road, some of the tension melted out of his shoulders, eased away by the softness of her leg under his fingertips, and he was distracted for a moment by the warmth of her creamy skin. He'd spent his adult life running away from women before they could leave him. No attachment. No heartache. But the redheaded spitfire beside him had changed all that.

Claire sucked in a breath, pulling his gaze toward her. Confusion and desire battled in her eyes. She opened her mouth, but turned her head at the phone's jingle, announcing it was ready. She waited a moment longer, then dialed 911.

"I want to report a fire at Harvest Bistro, 6522 Main Street... No, no one's inside." Her tight voice broke. "Please hurry."

She hung up and immediately dialed again.

"Hank, it's Kendall's father, she was blackmailing him."

While she gave her brother the details, Jake kept his eyes on the road as Dry Creek disappeared behind them. It was a straight shot to the airport. The SUV wasn't built for speed, but it barreled down the highway like a rocket-powered tank. His headlights illuminated the idle sugar beet factory and closed big-box stores on either side of the highway. He glanced over at her alabaster skin lit up by the dashboard's green light.

She waved her free hand in the air as she argued with Hank. "No, we are not waiting for you. The sheriff's office is half an hour from the airport; by the time you get here he could be gone. We can't take that risk. Just meet us there. Hurry!"

Unable to turn away from the stubborn set of her jaw, he didn't realize the SUV had wandered onto the shoulder until the vehicle started to shake as he drove over the edge of the roadway. He yanked the steering wheel and got the SUV back on the highway. Adrenaline surged through his body as the vehicle fishtailed on the pavement. Both hands on the wheel, he regained control of the vehicle and his desperate thoughts in time to make the turn into the airport.

A few empty cars dotted the parking lot; among them was Burlington's sedan. The single terminal was wrapped in darkness, but through the chain-link fence surrounding the airfield, he spotted a small white jet idling on the tarmac. Burlington.

"Wait here for Hank." Jake flicked off the engine, shot out of the SUV and made a beeline toward the fence.

Burlington could fly away at any moment. Jake jumped onto the fence and started climbing. It swayed under his weight while he scrambled up. The jet engine purred in the background as he sailed over the top and dropped to the tarmac.

A second set of footsteps slapped the ground behind him and he spun around, ready to confront an attacker.

Claire stood barefoot on the inside of the fence. Grunting, she tugged at the hem of her dress.

"Stupid thing is caught." She gave it a ferocious yank and the fabric tore free. Tumbling back, she came to a stop flat on her ass.

The rip in her dress extended up to her round hip. A flash of green thong caught his eye as she stood up and brushed herself off. Even in the midst of all this madness, his body responded with a lust that sucked the oxygen right out of his lungs and the blood from his brain.

"Stop staring at me like a dog eyeing a juicy steak." She smacked him on the arm. "We have to figure out how to stop that plane."

Hand-in-hand, they sprinted to a small wooden equipment shed. Peeling red paint flaked off onto Jake's shirt as he leaned against the shed. Eyeballing the plane, he absentmindedly brushed the paint off onto a pile of crumbled paint chips that had accumulated like a snowdrift alongside the shed. Claire wiped away the dust caked on its lone window and pressed her face against the glass.

"How long until Hank and his deputies get here?" Jake whispered and slid his body closer to Claire's, his muscles taut.

She pulled back from the window, dirt smudges darkening her nose and forehead. "At least twenty minutes. The sheriff's office is on the other side of town."

"No one was in the area?"

"This is Dry Creek, Jake. There are only three deputies on duty during the overnight shift and they're all at headquarters for shift change. That's why I told Hank we couldn't wait for him."

Jake grimaced and grasped for the inkling of a plan. It didn't even have to be a great one, just good enough to keep Burlington from jetting off to Brazil.

Bracing himself for the worst, he risked another glance around the shed. About fifty feet long, the small jet idled with its steps extended out to the tarmac. No one stood in the gangway or behind one of the plane's five windows. Desperation growing, he scanned the area near Burlington's jet in a clockwise circle, weighing the possibilities of each item crossing his line of vision. A moveable staircase. Two closed airplane hangars. A bright yellow crop duster.

Gas tankers parked beside each other at the far end. The glass doors to the terminal. A baggage car. Another equipment shed.

His body stiffened and he dragged his gaze back to the baggage car. Of course. Excitement pulsed through his body as he ducked his head back behind the shed. "There's a baggage car. I can smash it into the plane's staircase."

"Are you nuts?" Claire's voice cracked. "You want to play chicken with a jet?"

He swiped the grime from her nose with his thumb. "You got a better idea?"

She leaned forward and brushed an electric kiss across his lips. "No. But I know where the keys are." With an impish grin, she pointed toward the window.

Sure enough, a set of keys hung from a hook under a hand-printed sticky note reading, *baggage cart*. Elated, he grabbed her hand and they snuck around the corner to the shed's door. His body tense, prepared for an attack, he twisted the knob as he watched the jet. The door swung open and hit the wall with a thud.

They darted inside the shed's gloomy interior lit only by the airport's floodlights. The dust covering everything tickled Jake's nose. Claire snatched the keys. The daredevil gleam in her eyes scared him down to his toes. He needed to get those keys quick before she decided she'd be the one to ram Burlington's plane.

"Oh, no you don't." He held out his hand for the keys.

A shadow slunk across the wall beside Claire. Too late, Jake's inner alarm bells clanged. Goose bumps popped up along his arms. The summer breeze changed direction and cigar smoke wafted into the shed.

The color drained from Claire's face as she looked past his shoulder.

Heart pumping at breakneck speed, he spun around.

Franklin.

A makeshift white gauze bandage covered one eye, but hate glistened in the other. The big man spit out his lit cigar, cracked his knuckles and pointed at Jake. "You're all mine."

Claire gasped.

Operating purely on instinct, he hurled himself at the huge goon, pushing him out of the doorway. "Run, Claire!"

Her bare feet smacked against the tarmac as she cleared the doorway. Jake steamrolled Franklin, pushing him around the shed's corner. They jostled for control, punching and grappling.

With a low growl, the big man slammed his head against Jake's forehead. Pain spiraled through his skull and everything went black. Unable to defend himself, Franklin's punch to the gut sent Jake to the ground on top of a pile of paint chips.

"I am going to enjoy my time with that little lady." Franklin drove his cruel words home with a kick to Jake's side.

His body screamed in agony, but his sight returned. Everything had a fuzzy glow to it, but he could see. The red flakes scattered on the ground in front of him made his lips curl back into a snarl. When it came to saving Claire, Jake wasn't above fighting dirty.

Franklin stood, watching Claire as she dashed toward the baggage cart. Jake would be damned before he let Franklin harm a single strand of auburn hair on her head.

Letting out a yowl of fury, Jake swung out one leg and swept the goon off his feet. The big man landed with a thump on the tarmac. Quick as a tornado rips through a trailer park, Jake grabbed a handful of paint chips and ground them into Franklin's good eye. The thug howled as he pawed at his injury.

Jake struggled up, his lungs heaving and head pounding. He turned in time to see Claire at the helm of the baggage cart headed straight for Burlington's jet on the opposite side of the tarmac. She was going to get herself killed.

Sprinting toward her, he second guessed his every move since he'd arrived in Dry Creek. He'd doubted Burlington's story about the phone's and flash drive's importance since the beginning, but he'd ignored his better judgment. When Burlington threatened his dad, he'd almost turned on Claire. Since he'd met her, she'd been beaten up, had her home trashed, her body drugged, her restaurant torched and now this.

Sprinting toward her, he fought past the pain cramping his side and the burning in his lungs with each ragged breath. Terror wrenched his heart apart. He'd never reach her before she smashed into the jet.

ഗ്ഗ

The steering wheel shook in Claire's grasp as she bounced across the baggage cart's seat. If the vehicle had shocks, they'd been worn off years ago and never replaced. Ignoring the beating her tailbone was taking from the jostling cart, she drove hell bent for leather toward the plane's lowered staircase.

Tires screeched on the tarmac. The cart tipped as the right-side tires lifted off the ground and the trailer, normally filled with travelers' luggage, weaved like a snake behind her.

Claire held her breath and squeezed her eyes tight, waiting for the whole thing to roll. For a millisecond, she thought it was all over, but the thunk of the tires hitting the ground proved her wrong. Air whooshed out of her lungs. Tonight, she loved being wrong.

The landing threw her body up in the air, but she held on to the steering wheel for dear life. As soon as her butt hit the hard plastic seat, she hunched over the wheel and pushed the gas pedal to the floor.

"Claire!" Jake's voice rose above the baggage cart's rattling.

She snapped her head around in his direction. He waved his arms over his head as he dashed toward her. Franklin, the rat bastard, squirmed on the ground behind Jake. The goon had curled up in the fetal position next to the shed. Good riddance to bad rubbish.

Jake had done his part. Now it was her turn. Stiffening her shoulders, she focused in on the plane. Only open tarmac stood between her and the staircase. A shadow appeared in the plane's doorway. Burlington. A second later, the stairs started to fold upward.

She leaned forward, willing the baggage cart to go faster, but the little engine was already giving her its all. Her heart sank. He couldn't get away now, not when they were so close. Halfway up, the stairs stilled, just the kind of lucky break she needed. She had to aim just right. If she could damage the stairs, Burlington wouldn't be able to close the door to take off.

Police sirens wailed in the background. Hank and his backup were almost there. They were going to do it. Burlington wouldn't get away.

The stairs dropped a foot, stuttered, then climbed upward again. Heart hammering in her chest. The stairs cranked up higher and higher. Just as the last step was slightly lower than the cart's hood, she rammed into the stairs.

The force of the crash slammed her chest into the steering wheel. Waves of pain undulated from her sternum as her head snapped forward. The screech of metal scraping metal reverberated down her spine. Gasping for breath, she locked her fingers around the steering wheel, afraid of being tossed from the cart. Finally, the world stopped zooming by. The stairs were to damaged to close, she'd accomplished her mission.

Hands grabbed at her, pulled her from the seat. Disoriented, she ineffectually slapped at the hard, muscular chest swimming in front of her.

"If you ever do that again, I swear to God I'll never sit center ice with you at a hockey game." Jake enveloped her in his arms.

Warmth that had nothing to do with the summer heat swamped her body as she melted into him. Wrapped in his solid embrace, Claire regained her bearings as sheriff's deputies surged onto the runway with their cruisers' lights flashing.

Hank burst out of one of the cars, his gun pointing toward the plane. Burlington stood at the top of the stairs. Without a fight, Burlington raised his hands, surrendering to the inevitable.

Claire sighed into Jake's chest. She felt as if she'd gone twelve rounds in the ring with the heavyweight boxing title holder. Pushing her own aches and pains to the background, she focused on the damage Franklin had inflicted on Jake. Wincing at the sight, she took in his bloodied nose and the shiner darkening his left eye.

"You look like you just *played* in a hockey game."

He smirked down at her and patted her wind-twisted hair. "Yeah, we make a hell of a couple."

"We sure do." She wrapped her arms around his neck and captured his lips with hers. Activity swirled around them, but her bones dissolved and her muscles became limp. Right now, there was only Jake.

His hands slid up her sides, rubbing against the ache throbbing in her ribs. Claire jerked back from the kiss, panting in agony. Black dots marred her vision and she waited for the searing pain to lessen.

"Shit, Claire. We've got to get you to the ambulance. Come on." Jake scooped her up into his arms and hustled her over to the waiting medics.

She kept her breaths short and shallow in an effort not to aggravate her sore ribs. But her misery must have flashed on her face like a neon sign because the paramedic took one look at her and waved her inside the vehicle. Jake helped her up and took a seat in the stretcher across from her.

"Sit up, don't lie down." The EMT slid his palms down her side. His assessing touch was gentle, but when he connected with the rib underneath her right breast, she writhed in agony and squirmed back from him.

He shook his head and sighed. "It could be a bad bruise or a fracture. We'll have to take you in."

Jake grabbed her hand. His gaze didn't waver from her when his phone started ringing.

"Go on, answer it. I don't think we have to worry about phone calls anymore." Claire tried to smile, but the effort exhausted her.

He squeezed her fingers and answered the phone with his free hand. "Hello?"

His grasp on her fingers tightened until their tips were almost purple. With care, she slid them away, knowing from the pinched look on his face that something else had gone wrong.

What now? It had to be over. Burlington was in custody. Tears sprang to her eyes, she couldn't take any more bad guys.

"I'll be there as soon as I can." He nodded once and clicked the phone off.

She leaned forward, ignoring her throbbing ribs, to take his hands in hers. "What now?"

"It's my old man." A distant, mournful look haunted his slate-blue eyes. "He's having trouble breathing. They don't think it's related to his lung cancer, but they can't be sure. They just took him to the hospital. I'm sorry, Claire, I have to get back to Denver."

The despondent look on his face hurt her more than the steering wheel to her ribs had. "Go on. You don't need to come to the hospital with me. Go home to Denver." She brushed his lips with hers, her heart aching for him.

He returned her gentle kiss before she pulled away. He slid his thumb across her swollen lips, worry and regret plain in his gaze. "Claire, I..." His hands fell to his sides. He opened and shut his mouth a few times, but no more words came.

"It's okay, Jake. Everything will be okay." Her bottom lip trembled as she dug her fingernails into her palms, hoping her words made it true.

He stood, hunched over, in the crowded ambulance and shuffled out. As he straightened to his full height in the parking lot, he turned. The torment etched on his face twisted her into a knot.

He plowed his fingers through his short black hair. "I...we...this..."

The knot tightened until her heart tore in two. This was it. He wasn't coming back. They'd known a relationship wasn't in the cards. Whatever they were doing, it wouldn't last past his time in Dry Creek. Now that time was up. He'd probably remember the past few days as just a crazy interlude brought about by the chaos they'd experienced.

Part of her wanted to plead her case, beg him to love her as much as he said. But she couldn't add to the stress and pressure he was no doubt feeling right now.

She swallowed hard against the lump in her throat. Best for both of them to let him off the hook now.

"Don't worry about me. I'll be fine from here on out on my own thanks to you." She took in a shaky breath. "Jake, go be with your dad. He needs you."

He remained still for another few seconds, shoulders slumped and his face turned toward the ground. When he looked up, a hollowness darkened his gaze. Then, he spun around on his heel and strode for the gate.

Wondering if she'd really done the right thing, Claire watched him go until the EMT shut the doors and the ambulance took off.

Chapter Seventeen

*G*iggles, interrupted by the occasional high-pitched squeal, erupted from the other side of the hospital door. Curious, Jake peeked through the rectangular window into his father's recovery room and smiled.

Absolute Security's longtime secretary, Velma, sat on his dad's bed, her hand clamped over her mouth, while the old man waved a spoonful of lemon-yellow Jell-O in her direction. They'd been acting like goofy teenagers for the past six months, ever since Velma told his stubborn father that she was getting married. It wasn't until after the old man finally declared his love for her that Velma admitted there was no fiancé. Ever since, Jake had been catching them kissing in the copy room, sneaking out early for matinees and making cow eyes at each other. It was sickening. And sweet. Not that he'd ever say that to them.

Pushing open the door, Jake smothered his grin. "Okay. Break it up, you two. I've got the car out front to take you home."

Velma jumped from the bed and smoothed her floral skirt over her ample thighs. A smile so big it made her dimple seem miles deep lit up her face. "Hey there, Jake."

The old man turned a scowl Jake's way and grunted in greeting. When Velma had called Jake last night, no one knew what was wrong. Turned out to be a respiratory infection. The doctors had wanted to keep him in the hospital for longer than overnight, but, par for the course, the old man ignored their advice.

"Damn, Velma, I told you not to call him. Now I have to deal with a son who thinks he's my boss."

Jake shook his head. "Trust me, no one wants that job."

Velma leaned down and brushed the old man's lips with hers. "Sugar, I'm heading back to the office and I don't want to see you there for at least a week."

"A week," his father sputtered. "That place will go to pot without me for a week."

Velma raised a penciled eyebrow at him. The old man shut his trap.

"Love you, baby," she hollered over her shoulder and strode out the door.

His father climbed out of the bed and stood on spindly legs. "Tell me you brought me something to wear so I don't have to flash my ass to the world."

Ten minutes later they were in Jake's SUV, headed for his dad's house. Traffic was a bitch. They were stuck behind a minivan at a light when the old man turned in the passenger seat to eyeball Jake.

"What?"

"When were you going to tell me about Burlington trying to blackmail you?"

Sighing, Jake considered his answer carefully. "Probably never."

"Mmm-hmmm. And what about the girl?"

"What girl?"

He crossed his arms. "Don't treat me like I'm stupid, Jake Allen Warrick. You haven't been able to fool me ever."

The light changed and Jake followed the minivan into the intersection. He drove in silence for another three blocks with his father staring a hole into his head. Damn, he never should have told Velma about Claire. Of course she'd told his dad. But it was too late. Claire didn't need someone like him. Knuckles whitening, he gripped the steering wheel tight and tried to ignore the pain eating him up inside.

"I'm still waiting for an answer." His dad coughed into a white handkerchief.

"Did Velma tell you?" He honked his horn at the slow-moving minivan. "I should have just kept my mouth shut."

"Doesn't matter how I found out. What I want to know is what you're going to do about it."

"Nothing. It's over."

"Bullshit." The old man spat out the word. "Do you love her?"

Remembering his declaration of love when he'd thought all was lost in Harvest, anger and regret burned through his veins. "She's better off on her own."

"That's not what I asked. Tell me the truth, do you love her?"

Yeah, he did, for all that it mattered. "No."

"You know what's worse than lying? Being too chicken to go after what you want. Be careful, son, it looks like there are feathers sprouting from your ears."

Caught at another red light, he whipped around in his seat to face his old man. "Oh yeah? That's worse than being too blinded by love or lust or whatever the hell happened to you with my mother to see you were chasing after someone who didn't want you? Who never wanted me? Are you so bitter that you want to see me make the same stupid, bullheaded mistake *you* made?" His hands shook with rage. "Claire told me she'd be all right on her own. I've already lived through the fallout of holding on to someone who doesn't want me. I don't need to do it again."

His father sighed, looking every bit like the exhausted cancer patient he was. "At one time, your mother did love me. We loved each other. But I got caught up in building Absolute Security, took her for granted. I felt her slipping away little by little. It started with her reading the paper at dinner instead of asking me how my day went. Then before I knew it, she was sleeping in your room, claiming she worried about how much you were coughing at night." Pausing, he glanced out the window. "I could have stopped it from going so wrong, but instead I ignored the ugly mess of our marriage. So did she, with the help of Jack Daniel's. And then by the time she walked away from us, it was too late to save even your relationship with her."

A heavy silence fell. Jake tried to process his old man's revelation that opened so many long-buried scars.

His father closed his eyes and slowly shook his head. When he opened his eyes, tears glistened, making their blue depths sparkle. "What happened between your mother and I, well, I'm sorry for it. But you can't let the mistakes she and I made dictate how you live your life."

"I'm not." Jake returned his gaze to the road and he crossed the intersection.

"So I'll ask you again—do you love her?"

Clenching his jaw, Jake glared at the road, refusing to acknowledge his dad's question. She didn't want him. Fine. He'd be damned if he tried to force himself into her life where, as her brother had rightly pointed out, he didn't belong. He pulled into the old man's driveway and turned off the engine.

"So that's it? You'll just walk away with your tail tucked between your legs?"

An angry heat sizzled though his body. "That's not what I'm doing."

"Damn straight you are. You're giving up." His father slung open the door and got out. "If you love her, you fight for her. And if you aren't man enough to do that, then I sure did a piss-poor job of raising you." He slammed the door and stomped to the house.

ও৵ও৵

Claire sank back into her pillows, her bedroom curtains shut tight, blocking out the midday sun. The pair of pain relievers she'd swallowed would soon dull the ache of her quickly healing bruised ribs so she could drift off into another unsatisfying nap.

Surrounded by a box of tissues, her silver cordless phone, the remote control, her cellphone and an empty carton of chocolate-brownie-chunk ice cream, she stared at the flickering images from a procedural cop show playing on the small television next to her dresser. It was the fifth episode she'd watched of an all-day marathon. She couldn't remember a single moment of the earlier episodes.

The heartbroken funk swamping her had rendered the show white noise.

Swiping at the dark stain dotting her yellow tank top, she decided it must be from last night's ice cream snack. Or had it been the hot chocolate from the previous morning? Who knew? She'd been wearing the same top and black yoga pants for three days. What did it matter what she wore? It wasn't as if she were going to work.

Rubbing salt into her wounds, she grabbed the week-and-a-half-old local paper from the nightstand. A huge full-color photo on the front page showed flames shooting from Harvest's roof while firefighters sprayed it with water. The headline above it read, *Arson Destroys Restaurant in Historic Building*.

In a flash of anger, she crumpled the paper and hurled it across the gloomy room.

There was no more Harvest for her to go to and forget her shredded heart. Nope, she was only going from her bed to the bathroom to the fridge. Burrowing deeper beneath the blankets, she closed her eyes, hoping for a dream that didn't involve watching Jake walk away.

She'd called him at his office the day after he'd left. His father's hospitalization had been a cautionary move for a respiratory infection. They'd released him the morning after Jake arrived in Denver.

He'd made a vague promise to call again soon and hurried off the phone. It was over. The certainty of it washed over her like a tidal wave, its undertow pulling her out into a sea of misery.

Still, she waited by the phone, willing it to ring. It had. Her mom, brothers and Beth had checked in on her on a regular basis. They'd rung her doorbell and pushed their way inside, but she'd shooed them away, secretly expecting Jake to call. But he never did.

A few greasy strands of unwashed hair snuck out of her ponytail and tickled her cheek. Annoyed, she tucked the strands behind an ear as her heavy eyelids slid closed. Maybe she should take a shower. She would, as soon as she woke up.

Before she even had a chance to settle into a REM state, bright light burst into the room.

"Clarabell Anne Layton, I have had quite enough of this. I hereby declare your pity party officially over. Get out of bed and into the kitchen. I've got a non-chocolate, non-ice cream lunch waiting for you." Her mom, Glenda, stood in front of the window, having yanked up the blinds. A motherly look of exhausted patience clear on her face as she walked across the hardwood floor and to the bedroom door.

Claire flipped the pillow over her head. "Mom, let me be."

"You have five minutes to get your butt into the kitchen or else I'm sending your father in here to watch the game. He forgot his hearing aid at home, so the TV will be blaring loud enough to rattle your teeth, but if you'd rather stay in here, so be it." Her footsteps tapped out the door. "Your time starts now."

Claire groaned into the mattress. Her mom would send her dad in, no doubt with a bag of plain potato chips. He'd mumble at the television and elbow her to watch an instant replay.

"I have homemade macaroni and cheese baked with breadcrumbs on top," her mom hollered from the kitchen.

Stomach growling, Claire sat up and swung the covers off. Candy wrappers that had been laying on top of the blanket flew across the room. Her ice cream spoon clattered on the floor. Yeah. It was time to get out of bed.

In the kitchen, Onion dogged Glenda's feet as she took the glass casserole dish from the oven, pivoted and lowered her heavy load onto a trivet on the island. The dog's fat, pink tongue lolled from the side of his mouth as he sniffed the melted cheese aroma hanging in the air. There was no mistaking the greedy hope shining from his eyes. Good luck. Her mom was notoriously stingy when it came to feeding people food to dogs.

Glenda spooned some steaming macaroni and cheese into a white bowl. "Well, go get a fork. It's always better when the cheese is still melty."

Claire did as told and sat down on a wooden stool by the island. Her shoulders slumped, she dug into the cheesy goodness. Its warmth radiated outward from her stomach, a welcome relief to days of junk food. She didn't look up from her bowl until she'd polished off its gooey contents.

Her mother's no-nonsense glare froze her to the hard seat.

"I know you've been through a lot, young lady, but moping around your house smelling like a gym sock isn't going to fix anything." Glenda quirked an eyebrow. "So what's the plan?"

Claire sighed. She'd been trying to figure that out for days now. Which disaster did she want to deal with first? Harvest? Jake? Right now it hurt too much to try to tackle either heartache. "I don't know, Mom."

Glenda opened her mouth, but snapped it shut when the phone started ringing.

Grateful for the reprieve, Claire slid off the stool and grabbed the receiver. "Hello?"

"I'm looking for a...uh...Claire Layton." The man's cough rattled through the line. "She in?"

"I'm Claire, who's this?"

"Francis Warrick, Jake's dad. I want to know what the hell you did to my son."

Blood pounded in her ears at the audacious statement from a man she'd never met. "What I did to him?" she stammered.

"Oh hell, that came out all wrong," he wheezed. "But he won't tell me a damn thing, and he's acting as mean as a cat that got poked in the eye with a stick."

He was miserable, too? Maybe she had been wrong. Her heartbeat sped up. "So you figured you'd just call me up and use your silver tongue to get the scoop, huh?"

He chuckled. "Yeah, I'm not known for my people skills." His chest rattled as his laughter set off a coughing fit.

The sound pained her. "How're you feeling, Mr. Warrick?"

"Like shit, but that's the way it goes." He paused. "Look, we don't know each other, but my boy's a mess. If you two can't fix this, I might have to off him just to give myself some peace during my last days on this earth."

Claire had no idea what to say. His words sent hope burbling up from her toes, straightening her spine and energizing her weary body. Jake missed her. What other explanation was there? "Mr. Warrick..." Excited possibilities swirled around in her head, but no more words came. The silence grew as static crackled though the line.

"Yeah, well, I've said my piece." He cleared his throat. "So think about what I've said. Goodbye."

Staring down at the silent phone, uncertainty floated in her chest. She loved him, but was that enough? He'd walked away so easily from her.

Questions she couldn't answer rocketed around her head as she hung up the phone. No matter what she did, she risked heartbreak, but only one choice came with big rewards.

Claire pivoted to face her mom. "That was Jake's dad. He said Jake is a wreck."

"Of course he is. There's something about falling for a Layton that will really throw you for a loop, make you rethink your life." Glenda covered the casserole dish in plastic wrap and slid it into the refrigerator.

Curiosity piqued, Claire walked back to the island. Her parents had had the perfect romance, from the stories her mom used to tell after one too many eggnogs on their Christmas Eve wedding anniversary. "But, you've always said it was love at first sight."

"That doesn't mean it was all smooth sailing." Glenda leaned against the refrigerator, a soft smile curving her lips. "I was about to graduate college and become the next Barbara Walters when I met him. We were waiting for the Greyhound bus to go home from school for the Christmas holiday. I noticed him standing in line at the ticket window. He was so tall, with honey-brown hair."

The man in question, now with hardly any hair, whooped and clapped in the living room. The game must be going well.

"Well, it was a long, boring ride, and I figured a cute boy would liven it up. I finagled it so we'd sit next to each other. Eight hours later, I knew I was not going to be the next Barbara Walters. I was going to be the next Mrs. Layton."

"Just like that you gave up your dream? Don't you regret that?"

Her mom sat down on the stool next to Claire. A dreamy look of nostalgia eased away the deep grooves in her forehead. A small smile tugged at the corners of her pink lips. "I didn't give up anything. I gained everything."

"But..." Claire's words evaporated when her mother shook her head.

"It may not have been New York, but I sat behind the WOMD news desk for twenty years. I loved that job until the day I retired. In place of a big city, I got your father, your brothers, you and a lifetime of happy memories."

Glenda slapped her palms on the island, pushed herself up from the stool and exhaled a deep breath. "What you think you want from life isn't always what you really need. You just have to be smart enough to figure out the difference between a Brett and a Jake." She swiped Claire's empty bowl from the island and carried it to the sink. "The question is, do you have the gumption to get your stinky self into the shower and then go track down that fella?"

Claire gazed out her kitchen window at the empty spot where Jake had parked his SUV the night of the storm. Stubbornly, she'd fought against it, but she'd known that night. Just like it had happened with her parents, something had clicked into place when she met Jake. She could trust him with her life and her heart.

Jumping down from the stool, she dashed across the kitchen to the sink and sidled up behind her mother, wrapping her arms around her in a bear hug. "Thanks, Mom."

Her mom shimmied out of her grasp. "You're welcome. Now go take that shower before I keel over."

❧❧❧

The yellow low-gas light blinked to life on Jake's dashboard as he pulled into the convenience store. He'd cut it closer than he'd have liked, but he'd been in such a hurry to hit the road, he hadn't filled up the tank before leaving Denver.

The phone on the black leather passenger seat began vibrating as he turned off the engine. Scooping it up, he saw the old man's cellphone number on the caller ID. "So what's the word?"

He held his breath. His whole plan rested on surprising Claire and catching her off guard. He feared she wouldn't answer the door if she knew he was on the other side.

"Hello to you too." The old man paused. "She's home. Told her you were as surly as a mean drunk on a four-day bender."

Jake rolled his eyes. "Thanks, Dad."

"Yeah, well, that's what you get when you ask me to act as an intermediary. You want soft and lovely, find someone else," he rasped. "You want the truth, you come to me. And you've been a pain in the ass."

Shaking his head, Jake smiled despite himself. "Thanks for making the call. I'm sorry, Dad, I know the timing of this is all wrong..." What type of son would leave his father after he'd just gotten out of the hospital? "Maybe it can wait."

"Only if you want me to crack you upside the head with my oxygen tank," the old man grumbled. "Oh hell, I'll still be dying tomorrow, but I can't promise that girl will be willing to give you another chance tomorrow. You've got today."

A tank full of gas later, Jake got back on the road. He had a forty-minute drive to figure out how to make Claire take him back.

ço·ço·ço

Claire swiped her pruney fingers across the bathroom mirror, clearing away the steam that had fogged it up. She'd taken longer than she'd wanted, but then again, she'd had three days' worth of pity party to scrub away. Inhaling the vanilla scent of her body butter, she quickly rubbed it into her smooth legs, eager to finish and get to Denver. Squeezing the extra wet out of her hair, she decided to let it air dry a bit before blowing it dry.

After making sure the fluffy white towel was secured in place around her body, she stepped out into the hallway. Onion lounged in the middle of the hall, a paw peddling the air as he slept in the too quiet house.

Claire peeked around the corner. Her dad wasn't asleep on the couch. The television wasn't on. "Mom. Dad. You here?"

Walking over to the bay window to check for their car, she spotted a note on the coffee table. *Bingo night. Drive safe. Love, Mom and Dad.* She let the note fall back to the table and turned to get dressed. A knock at the door stopped her. Mom must have forgotten her lucky bingo markers.

A smart remark about bingo addiction ready on the tip of her tongue, she yanked opened the door. Her heart stopped.

Jake glowered at her from the front porch.

Chapter Eighteen

*C*laire's breath caught and her heart went into overdrive. Coiled tension rolled off of his hard body in waves that crashed over her exposed skin. Knees weakened, she leaned her shoulder against the door, its plywood covering scratching her shoulder. Neither said a word as the air sizzled around them.

Something she couldn't pinpoint simmered in his slate-blue eyes as he tugged on the edge of his wrinkled blue T-shirt. It looked as if he'd slept in the cotton shirt that was partly tucked into the waistband of his snug jeans. He shoved his hands into his pockets and locked his gaze on her.

"You're stubborn, pushy and impulsive. I have a life of my own in Denver. It's a good life." Despite his quiet tone, the low timbre of his voice hinted at his frustration. He closed the distance between them until his heat seeped through her towel. "I didn't want to want you."

His harsh words punched a hole in her heart. Closing her eyes, she bit down on her bottom lip and fought the tears pooling behind her lids. If it wasn't for the door holding her up, she would have sunk into a puddle on the floor. A hand under her chin tilted her face upward, sending unwanted sexual sparks through her body.

"Open your eyes, Claire." His warm breath whispered across the sensitive skin of her ear. "Look at me. Please."

Warmth fled from her skin when he stepped back. She gathered her strength. Best to just get it over with and get him out of here. She'd be damned if she'd let him see how much his admission hurt.

Bracing herself for the devastation ahead, she opened her eyes. Hope was the last thing she expected to see in his gaze.

"The past week and a half without you has been hell. When I came to Dry Creek, I didn't want to want you. But I was a real dumbass for thinking that." Running a hand through his disheveled black hair, Jake sighed. "You're everything I need." His voice broke and he gulped before going on. "I love you, Claire Layton, and I'm not going anywhere, so you'd better get used to it."

He loved her. He. Loved. Her. Mounting exhilaration buzzed inside her with such force, she wouldn't have been surprised to see sparks fly out of her fingertips. "And you think I'm pushy?"

Laughter erased his worry lines. A devilish smirk curled his lips and he tweaked her on the nose. "I think you're amazing." Squeezing two fingers into the top of the towel wrapped around her body, he tugged her closer. "I think you're beautiful." With a quick yank, he whipped the white cotton away. "I think you need to tell me you love me."

A warm summer breeze tickled her bare skin. Jake's big hands curved around her willing body and kneaded her ass, sending jolts of pleasure up her spine, making it hard to formulate a witty comeback. Her nipples pebbled against the soft cotton of his T-shirt as she realized she didn't need one. This was right. They were right together. "I love you. Now take me inside unless you plan on having sex on my front porch in full view of the cornstalks."

"Yes, ma'am." He scooped her up in his arms and strode through the house, deftly negotiating around Onion, still asleep in the hall.

Sneaking her hands under his shirt, she reveled in his taut abs twitching under her palms. Want overwhelmed her. This man was hers. To touch. To lick. To fuck. To love. So lost was she in her exploration, she didn't realize they were in her bedroom until Jake tossed her onto the freshly made bed. Easing herself up onto her elbows, she licked her lips as Jake peeled off his T-shirt.

Curling forward until she sat up, Claire ran her tongue across his stomach. The warm musk of his cologne enveloped her as she leaned back to focus on his low-slung jeans. Busy with his zipper, her gaze followed her fingers as she inched it lower. Realizing he'd gone commando ratcheted up her need; her clit strained with each tantalizing glimpse of springy, jet-black curls.

His cock sprang from confinement as she pushed his jeans over his lean hips, tempting her with the nearness of its engorged head. A frisson of anticipation skittered across her tender skin.

Jake's fingers tenderly twisted the hair at the nape of her neck. "Me first."

Gently, he nudged her onto her back then released her hair. Capturing her wrists in one hand, he stretched her arms above her head as far as they would go.

The position forced her breasts to jut upward, the twin peaks exposed and begging to be touched.

Nearly undone by the anticipation, a desperate moan escaped her yearning body.

He lowered his hot mouth and stroked them with his tongue, sending fire sizzling through her body. His teasing fingers circled her wet pussy as he continued his soft assault on her tingling nipples.

Back arched, her entire body pleaded for a harder touch on her clit. Needing to hold onto something solid, she twisted the comforter in her hands. "Please, Jake."

He chuckled into the valley between her breasts, his warm breath tickling her tensed nerves there. "What's wrong?" He punctuated his question by grazing the distended peach nipple with his teeth.

"More."

"More what?" He slowed his stroking fingers until it seemed her pussy would collapse with want. "Tell me what you want more of, Claire."

Pleasure ricocheted across her body, from the stretch of her arms to the yearning ache in her core. "Touch my clit, rub it harder."

He increased the pressure but kept the speed agonizingly slow. "Like this?"

The combination of pressure and unhurried pace stole her ability to form words. She moaned her assent, twisting her hips as a vibration started building in her thighs.

"Or is it more of this?" Hard and fast, two of his fingers whirled around her wet lips, dipping inside her steamy depths so his palm massaged her clit.

"Yes... That... Do that." Turning her head, she panted into the covers. The tremors in her legs deepened as the tightness in her pussy increased.

Everything built higher and tighter, her entire body heaving with need.

Just when she thought she couldn't take it any more, Jake pinched her clit, sending her over the edge. A strangled moan escaped as the orgasm exploded like an atom bomb. Aftershocks of pleasure rippled through her body. Jell-O had more consistency than her bones.

The bed dipped when Jake lay down next to her, pulling her pliant form against his unyielding frame. While she spooned with her back glued to Jake's chest, the world floated back into focus. He nuzzled the base of her neck, tickling her with his day-old beard. His long fingers strummed against her stomach, his thumb brushing her bellybutton. Although she'd yet to catch her breath, blood began rushing in response to the primitive chords he played.

The crinkle of ripping foil preceded him slipping on a condom. Like a lightning rod, his iron-hard cock nestled against her tight ass, focusing and attracting her sexual energy. Grinning wickedly, she swiveled her hips against him in easy, small circles. His hand slid down to her hip, locking her in place. He pushed against her, his cock driving between her slick folds from behind.

"Jake." Her voice, strangled with pleasure, pleaded with him as he filled her.

"You feel so good." His words were hot against her neck.

Her body responded to his rhythm, increasing the pace as need grew within her. His fingers glided through the skinny landing strip of tight curls around her pussy. When he made contact with her sensitive clit, her back bowed and fire shot through her body. A few revolutions around her already sensitive button and a spine-tingling sensation streaked up her back in a climax that reverberated across her body in a blaze of white light.

Jake flipped onto his back, taking her with him so she gyrated on top of him, facing away. Grinding her hips against him, she reached between his legs to cup his tight balls. His moan of encouragement spurred her on to take him in deeper until there was nowhere else for him to go. She leaned into a backbend, her back arched over his chest and her palms flat on either side of of him while riding his erection rough and hard.

Claire undulated upward. Jake followed into a sitting position, pushing her forward until she was on her hands and knees. Calloused fingers gripping her hips, he plunged into her soaking-wet core. She met each of his forceful thrusts, their bodies urging each other on toward that other dimension where pleasure bordered on the divine. Each forward motion of his cock rubbed against the spongy nerve endings deep within her, enticing her G-spot to the next level of hedonistic bliss.

She folded herself down onto her elbows, her ass high in the air, as Jake drove into her, his balls slapping against her bare flesh. The tempo increased to a frantic rhythm, ecstasy lying just beyond her reach. The pressure swelled until it consumed her. In an instant, the world shattered as her pussy convulsed around Jake's rigid cock. Jake shook as he plunged inside of her one last time, coming with her name on his lips.

They collapsed onto the twisted covers on her bed. Her lungs struggled for breath as her heart slowed to a less frenzied rate. Curled within his strong arms, Claire rested her cheek against the soft curls on his chest, exhausted and happy beyond belief.

Jake circled his palm on the small of her back. "I'm definitely never going now."

She snorted against his ribs. "Good, because there's no way I'd let you." Her heavy eyelids lowered and she surrendered to sleep, safe and warm in Jake's arms.

Epilogue

*M*uck sloshed over the pointed toe of Claire's knee-high leather boots. Great. She'd been trying to avoid the muddy puddles dotting Harvest's parking lot but had gotten distracted when Jake grabbed her hand. The moment their fingers touched, her body turned into a sea of molten want. Never mind that he'd left her satisfied and panting less than an hour ago. She needed more. Even after two months of spending nearly every day together, her lust for him hadn't lessened. Looking down at her gray, soaked boots, she admitted there was a downside to that.

"Hey, Claire, glad to see you on the site." Billy, the construction foreman, hurried to their side. Contemplating her wet shoes, he spit a brown stream of tobacco juice to the other side of them.

"You'll be even happier when you see this." She snatched her insurance check out of her purse and waved it underneath his nose.

"Hot damn." He rubbed his hands together. "So we're a go?"

"Yep. How soon can you start rebuilding?"

"The demolition's just about finished. It'll take us a few days to clear the site and then we'll get moving." Billy glanced back at what was left of Harvest. All that remained were piles of burnt wood and debris. "I'll let the guys know they've got a hell of a job ahead of them."

Claire leaned back against Jake's wide chest as Billy strode away. Glancing up at the building's charred remains, grief squeezed her heart, but not as tightly as before. Now that she had her insurance check, she was going to build again, make it better than it had been.

"Still think you can share an office with me and keep your panties on?"

She elbowed Jake in the gut. "Shhh. The guys will hear you."

"I thought that was your secret plan. Get me to open an Absolute Security satellite office in Dry Creek so you could have your wicked way with me anytime day or night."

The smirk on his face said he was joking, while the growing bulge pressing against her ass told a different story. One she'd like to read as soon as she could get him somewhere private. Her nipples hardened and her thighs tingled at the thought.

The chirp of her cellphone stopped her lascivious thoughts. Jake gave her a quick peck on the cheek and strolled across the parking lot toward the foreman. She reached for her phone buried in her purse. Man, he looked good walking away, but she liked watching him come better.

Pulling the phone out of her bag, she promised herself she'd make this a fast call. A number with a 702 area code flashed at her from the phone's screen. Where was that? Almost everyone she knew had a local phone number.

"Hello?"

"Claire, I think I'm in trouble." Panic tightened Beth's voice.

Tension cramped Claire's body. Beth was never in trouble. "Where are you? What's happened?" The questions rushed out of her mouth.

"I'm in Vegas." A heavy silence followed Beth's declaration.

Claire fought to keep her voice calm while visions of her best friend trapped in various dire situations flashed through her mind. "What happened? Did you gamble away your hotel money? Do you need bail? What is it?"

The blaring beep of a construction truck backing up overpowered Beth's mumbled answer. "What? I can't hear you, Beth. Speak up!" Claire sprinted away from the ruckus.

"I can't talk louder. He's in the bathroom. I had to wait for the shower to come on before I could call you." Beth's whispered words barely carried over the noise of the construction equipment.

"Who's in the shower? Who's he?" Had she been kidnapped? Claire's pulse went into hyperdrive and she pressed the phone hard against her ear.

"Claire, I think I married your brother."

"What?" Of all the scenarios, this was one she'd never expected.

"Oh God, the shower just turned off. What am I going to do?" Beth's apprehension vibrated through the phone line.

She couldn't make her friend's words make sense. Married? Her brother? The synapses in her brain finally connected.

"Beth," she screamed into the phone. "Which brother?"

A Note From Avery

Hey you!

I really hope you enjoyed Claire and Jake! They were the first romance couple I ever wrote and are still two of my favorite characters...even with Claire's crazy impulse control issues. :) If you have a second to leave a review of Dangerous Kiss, that would be awesome! And if you're dying to know which Layton brother Beth has maybe married, check out an excerpt of Dangerous Flirt.

Please stay in touch (avery@averyflynn.com), I love hearing from readers! Want to get all the latest book news? Subscribe to my newsletter for book gossip, monthly prizes and more!

And don't forget to check out the other Layton books: Dangerous Flirt and Dangerous Tease.

xoxo,

Avery

Books By Avery Flynn

The Killer Style Series
High-Heeled Wonder (Killer Style 1)
This Year's Black (Killer Style 2)
Make Me Up (Killer Style 3)

Sweet Salvation Brewery Series
Enemies on Tap (Sweet Salvation Brewery 1)
Hollywood on Tap (Sweet Salvation Brewery 2)
Trouble on Tap (Sweet Salvation Brewery 3)

Dangerous Love Series
Dangerous Kiss (Laytons 1)
Dangerous Flirt (Laytons 2)
Dangerous Tease (Laytons 3)

Novellas
Hot Dare
Betting the Billionaire
Jax and the Beanstalk Zombies (Fairy True 1)
Big Bad Red (Fairy True 2)

Newsletter

Subscribe to Avery's newsletter for news about her latest releases, giveaways and more!

Street Team

Join the Flynnbots and get sneak peeks at Avery's latest books and more!

Visit Avery's website at www.averyflynn.com

Facebook: https://www.facebook.com/AveryFlynnAuthor

TSU: https://www.tsu.co/AveryFlynn

Pinterest: https://www.pinterest.com/averyflynnbooks/

Twitter: https://twitter.com/averyflynn

E-mail: avery@averyflynn.com